BIRDS OF A FEATHER

A fortunate man, Sir Anthony Swale is married to a loyal wife; he lives in a grand house in Somerset and leads a very privileged life. He devotes most of his time to collecting rare art treasures, particularly from behind the Iron Curtain. And he will pay any price for the right piece — including treason. But then his treachery is discovered — and agents working for the Government decide it is time to take discreet action . . .

Books by Victor Canning
Published by The House of Ulverscroft:

THE BOY ON PLATFORM ONE

VICTOR CANNING

BIRDS
OF A
FEATHER

Complete and Unabridged

ULVERSCROFT
Leicester

First published in Great Britain in 1985

This Large Print Edition
published 2012

British Library CIP Data

Canning, Victor.
  Birds of a feather.
  1. Suspense fiction.
  2. Large type books.
  I. Title
  823.9'12–dc23

  ISBN 978–1–4448–1172–8

Published by
F. A. Thorpe (Publishing)
Anstey, Leicestershire
Set by Words & Graphics Ltd.
Anstey, Leicestershire
Printed and bound in Great Britain by
T. J. International Ltd., Padstow, Cornwall

This book is printed on acid-free paper

Birds of a feather flock together

Every man is as Heaven made him,
and sometimes a great deal worse.

Miguel de Cervantes: *Don Quixote*

1

Reaching the place where the cliff path broadened out into a wide bracken-free spread of close-cropped turf, Ruth Winslade sat down thankfully on the long seat which stood close to the National Trust collecting box set up to receive the offerings of tourists and walkers on their way up to and down from nearby Hurlstone Point. For a long time now it had been only rarely that she had made the walk to the top of the headland.

Behind her the ground ran broadly up the combe, the crozier shoots of young bracken now beginning to thrust above the winter-flattened old year's bronzed, dead growth. She loved the way the land swept broadly up to the heights of Bossington Hill and the small line of grey crags that hid the crest of distant Selworthy Beacon. She loved, too, the great spread of water before her of Porlock Bay, water which this morning was silvered by the sun from a cloudless sky. Distantly, farther along the Somerset coast, the great shoulder of Exmoor and the out-thrust of Countisbury Point glowed as though enamelled in soft green and burnt orange.

It was on such a morning as this that her husband had first brought her up here and — although their acquaintanceship had not been long — had proposed to her and she, through naïveté and inexperience, and with no gift then of reaching beyond appearances to the inner and persistent truth of another being's character, had accepted him. She smiled now as she thought of that raw girl of eighteen, sitting up here on a grass patch, inwardly trembling with a nameless emotion which was at once exhilarating and also daunting . . . for this man, ten years her senior, was a man of wealth and experience. No mark nor strain on her mind's image of him had she carried throughout their courtship days. She had lived as though in a dream. Mrs Harold Winslade . . . Harold Winslade of Highbury Park, a dream house, woodland and heath at its back and, skirting its small parkland, the twisting Avill brook running past Dunster in the east and then far beyond to find the sea.

Looking back over the years now she could be self-critical. If faults and abuse had lain mostly on Harold's side, there was also a lack of spirit, a weakness of will on hers, her inexperience of the world leading her at times to think that maybe this was the way some men . . . perhaps particularly those of great wealth and long endowed and esteemed family had, if not the right, at least the overbearing desire to behave. What an innocent she had been! And how immature. When she had distantly . . . oh, so distantly . . . made little more than the whisperings of complaint to her mother and then her father they had both — deliberately she knew now out of their total incapacity for dealing with such a bizarre situation — pretended it did not exist so far as they had allowed themselves to imagine the details of her complaints which she had far from baldly described. Today, she supposed, no girl would tolerate the situation and — thank God for progress — would have no hesitation in seeking out the right person and talking plainly.

Harold Winslade had been everything a husband should be — except for one thing. His sexual drive was a force inside him that was another person, another Harold Winslade. And this other Winslade, when it surfaced, as it too frequently did, was a monster of carnal appetite and gluttony.

He had been kind and gentle with her at first, since she was of no experience at all. And he had been in no hurry to widen her schooling. In a short time, though, she had begun to understand his nature, which was a combination of corruption and arrogance. Oh, frequent periods of kindness and loving concern he had shown, but these were more, she had come to understand, for the comforting of his own self-disgust. Later, his kindness and care withered. She was his. He fed, clothed and housed her well, bought her all she asked for and — perhaps his one saving grace — never humiliated or embarrassed her in company. No maid in the house was safe from him, and at some weekends he would bring guests who shocked and, to no little extent, sometimes frightened her.

She leaned back against her seat, sighed and shook her head at the folly and young bewilderment of herself in those days. The only time she was at peace and ease with him was when they walked or rode together, or when they were away from people. God knows, she took what happiness she could then . . . but it was not enough to hold any kind of balance against the days and nights at Highbury Park when he was down from London and the satyr in him cried out for and made dark revel.

She bore it until she was twenty-two — and would have borne it, perhaps, much longer (for the growth of her true spirit was a slow one), had he not one night, long after she had been alone in bed, come drunk to her room with a house guest, a woman friend of his from London. After all these years the scene was horribly clear in her memory, the sound of his voice and his evil suggestions never to be forgotten, nor her own sudden shuddering explosion of hatred and anger towards him. He had left her room and the next morning, without seeing her or giving any message for her, had returned to London with his guest.

He was away for two months and then one afternoon of early Spring had walked into her sitting room, which looked out over the terrace to the long meadow that ran down to the brook.

With unmoving features he had come to her, taken her hand and raised it to his lips in a brief dry kiss and then had said, 'I am a changed man. I crave from you forgiveness for all I have made you suffer in the past. I would that we were together again . . . if not, as yet, as full man and wife, then at least as companions and so from that to let come what may come.'

She had forgiven him. Watching now, far below, the black flight of a cormorant round the steep drop of Hurlstone Point, she could sincerely acknowledge that what he had proposed she welcomed. Did she not, the daughter of a clergyman, have a duty to offer every good will to help this man, her husband, fight and conquer the demon that lived within him?

She had taken him back and within four months he was as he had always been. The demon that possessed him had merely taken a holiday. And now, when he was sober he seemed to have forgotten all his excesses. But there were times when he was with her, both of them reading, when she would watch him over the edge of her book and see that his eyes stayed unmoving on some part of the page and that only at very long intervals did he turn a leaf and she knew that he was acting a part for her . . . and, God have mercy on him, she knew that there was some agony of soul in him for which there existed no relief.

A great tenderness was born in her for him and for the most part he responded to her care. But there was no stopping the occasional wildness. Maids left. He seldom went to London, though he saw to it that his affairs there and the estate here were run by his employees efficiently.

She leaned back against her seat, sighed with the weight of memory and looked at the steep drop a little higher up the path. The sight was as clear in her memory as it now was in her eyes. The tide was full in below and to the west lay the great run of beach to

Porlock. The air was full of the sound of seabirds calling. Courtship and nesting time. Man, beasts, birds . . . all moving to the great flux of new birth after winter.

He had come to her very early one morning and said, 'I'm told there are a pair of peregrine falcons nesting on Hurlstone Point. Let's go and have a look at them before other people will be about.'

So they had driven out, past Dunster and along the Porlock road, and then down through Allerford and West Lynch to Bossington. They left the car and crossed the little wooden bridge over the Aller and followed the river until they parted company, they to climb, and the river to find its way to the beach's great pebble ridge and beyond it the sea.

Although he had been full of talk in the car, from the moment they had crossed the river he was silent, walking a little ahead of her, but turning now and then to give a smile and raising in her a feeling that for some reason he was afraid of speech since it might betray him, weaken him from some resolve. Not until they were almost at the top of the path did he speak.

From where she sat now she could see the spot. It was a little way below the coastguard lookout building, hugging the cliff slope on

7

the right, falling almost sheer, first through gorse, bramble and bracken and then steep rock face. A small fence guarded the steep fall side now, but on that far-off morning there had been no fence.

He had stopped, turned, and given her a smile, and had said, 'No sign of the birds. But anyway they're around somewhere. That's what I'd like to have been . . . some bird or beast with no conscience. Just one drive — to stay alive and be what God made me . . . free from all sense of right or wrong. Now I go to my freedom and so — and this a last prayer — ensure yours and your happiness. Goodbye, my love.'

With a cry she had reached for him, but there was no saving him. At first, rather than falling, he had rolled awkwardly through thin bracken growth and low, looping briar brake until he reached the edge of a short shale side and then the cliff edge.

Thinking about it now, moved as she always was when the memory returned, she was surprised how so often some small piece of memory, part of the jigsaw of past emotion, came back to her. As her half-shout, half-scream died away a pair of jackdaws had called ruffianly and, it seemed, contemptuously from the farther headland rocks.

Looking at the fall now, she saw far below

and just off the headland the brief passage of some bird moving low across the water to be swiftly lost beyond the headland point. For a moment or two she fancied that it had been a peregrine falcon but could not believe it since it had been years since they had nested on the headland.

She turned away and began to move down the narrow path to find at the bottom of the slope the rough road which led up to the Aller ford and footbridge. The sycamore trees and bushes were all in young leaf. A chiff-chaff called incessantly. Now and again the water was briefly ringed with the rise of a small trout to take a fly. Since that loss . . . and she had come to acknowledge that it was a loss since there persisted at the back of her mind the suspicion that between them there could have been some salvation for him and a renewing of their marriage bonds . . . she had lived within the constraints of a regular life, a routine of days, weeks and months which slid by her known, foreseen, and — now more often than at any other time — increasingly . . . what? Boring? Placid? Undisturbingly predictable? All those years ago when he had taken his own life for her sake she had known and gone on facing the truth in her that her hand on her walking stick had tightened to force her into some action, some thrust or jab to send him over the cliff brink only to be stopped either — and the resolution of this would forever escape her — by her innate sense of right and wrong or a deep and loving pity for the lost creature whom life had overburdened with wild appetites and always-to-be-broken resolutions for reformation.

She came to the footbridge over the river and, crossing, saw waiting her chauffeur, Tom Honnicot, green jacketed and breeched, wearing a black peaked cap with a tiny rosette of furled silk over the shining visor . . . Tom Honnicot, shoulders squared and body ramrod stiff from years in the army and the dignity of a sergeant major still about him . . . Tom Honnicot who, on duty, worshipped correctness of behaviour and would have considered any blemish or untidiness in his turnout or that of the dark green Rolls-Royce as an offence to God and man and his mistress.

He stood to the rear door and opened it for her as she came up, put a finger to his cap in salute and, with a smile which to those who did not know him seemed more of a wince than a pleasantness of greeting, said, 'You had a good walk, ma'am?'

'Yes — thank you, Tom. I saw a fox going up the combe.'

'Aye, mum — there's an earth up the top there.'

'I think I saw something else, too.'

'Yes, ma'am?'

'Down below Hurlstone, coming round the point and low over the water . . . I'd have sworn it was a peregrine falcon . . . absolutely . . . a tiercel, too, I think. Thirty years ago I'd have thought nothing of it.'

'Nor me, ma'am. Thirty years ago it would have been nothing remarkable. Aye, and there's a lot of things like that — more's the pity. Not just things which have gone, but the ways that people have with one another. When I was a little tacker once . . . I got angry about something and swore at my mother. My old Dad heard — and that was it. Off come his great strap belt and I was over his knee and took ten of the best and no sitting down comfortably for a couple of days.' He grinned, and added, 'Learnin' you take in through your ears and eyes, but good manners stick longest after a hard belting.'

They drove back through Bossington and Lower Allerford to the main road, and then on through Dunster along the Exford road to Highbury Park. Half-way up the drive the car crossed the recently rain-swollen brook by a stone and ornately balustraded bridge. There had been a time, thought Ruth Winslade,

when she had imagined herself having a son
. . . had seen him in imagination fishing in the
brook . . . first with long-handled net for
bullheads, stickleback and minnows, and later
after trout with short rod and a dry fly . . . a
March Brown, a bit clumsily tied no doubt
under her initial tuition. Her father, after his
devotion to God and the Christian faith, loved
next the solitude of small stream trout fishing
and could quote the tying patterns of any
trout fly with the same ease as he could his
Bible . . . making each sound like some litany.
*Driffield Dun. Tail — pale ginger cock fibres.
Body — pale blue fur, ribbed yellow tying
silk. Wings — forward, pale starling. Hackle
— pale ginger cock.* She could have adopted
or early on remarried but had never had the
heart and courage to expose herself to the
possibility of more anguish or disappointment. When she died she would have no one
to whom she could leave the estate and her
wealth. Well, it would have to go to the
National Trust . . . though in her heart of
hearts, having nothing but admiration for the
Trust, she still was prejudiced in favour of
houses and land resting in private hands,
since then imagination and the idiosyncrasies
of individuals shaped dwellings and estates in
defiance of bureaucratically unimaginative
boundaries and strict economic functions.

The tiercel sat on a rock ledge a few feet above the high water mark at the foot of the Hurlstone Point cliff. He was in full, fresh Spring plumage . . . a shining blackish crown with bold cheeks and moustachial stripes, breast and under parts white tinged with buff and spotted and black barred below, cere and feet yellow, his beak dark blue. Four days ago he had left Kinsale Head on the coast of Ireland, where he had been raised the year before, and headed eastwards over the Irish Sea. His parent birds had disappeared during the winter and he was the sole progeny which had survived from the brood of three raised the previous year.

The drive to fly eastwards had not been strong. He had in fact almost loitered his way across, sometimes circling high under the sun and then coming down in mock stoop at some seabird. Mock, since he had no hunger, and no hunger because there was a different want stirring in his body.

He had found Hurlstone just as the last of the day's light was going and as he came in over the point he had stooped at one of a pair of jackdaws flying low along the great shingle stretch of Porlock bay where they had been foraging the beach drift left by the outgoing tide. He took the cock bird and carried it away to Hurlstone where he plucked and ate it.

The next morning he had seen the woman come up the coast path, had watched her sitting for some while and then, as she rose, he had winged out from the cliffs and turned eastwards around the point and out of her sight.

★ ★ ★

Margery Grant smiled to herself as she cycled down the farm lane at the sight of the open pick-up truck parked just the other side of the stone bridge which crossed the brook. Steve Black . . . Ever faithful, she thought. Ever hopeful, too. And with good cause to be . . . until it was all right and proper and with God's blessing. Though, of course, to keep it that way a girl had to look after herself and not let herself get carried away with moonlight and scrumpy. And anyway — her father would give her hell. Not the strap any longer. He'd given that up when her breasts had come. But there would be other ways. No dances, no pubs — just the chapel social and whist drives . . . Stuffy.

Steve Black stepped out into her road and held his hand up like a policeman. Tall, dark and handsome . . . knew it and when he could, traded on it — but not with her beyond what was in the Grant book of rules.

She got off her bike, gave him a *hello* and took a brief kiss on her cheek. He lifted the machine into the back of the truck and then handed her up into her seat. Which was something she always liked. He had — compared with most of the farmers' sons around here — good manners.

'Where to — the Swale place?'

'This time every week, as you know.'

''Course I do. Just like to flavour the taste of it. Give you a lift — that's a twenty-minute ride taken down to five minutes driving. Result. Fifteen minutes of Paradise with a capital P.'

'My Dad says you talk too much to be any good.'

'Your Dad's usually right. But with that one he's wrong.'

A few minutes later he pulled into a lay-by off the Exford road, gave her a quick kiss on the cheek before she had time to resist, and then said, 'If you don't want it — you can give it back to me.'

She laughed and said, 'One day you'll talk yourself into real trouble.'

He suddenly frowned and said, 'They say, you know, that he beats Lady Swale. Spends most of his time in London and just comes down when he feels the need to give her a good hiding for something she hasn't done nor never thought of doing. Sorry for the nor never.'

'Why?'

'Purity of speech. My old man's a farmer. But he was a schoolmaster for years before he realized that sheep were easier to handle than scruffy schoolboys and, also, that there was more money in it. Why don't you marry me? You could cook for Dad and me and we'd have the attic bedroom. Aunt Dora wouldn't mind — she'd have more time for gardening and have a hammock in the greenhouse and — '

'Shut up.'

'Why?'

'Because I don't like some of your joking. Particularly about Lady Swale. She's one of the nicest ladies I know.'

'I never said she wasn't. It's him I can't stand. I reckon one day she'll run off with that Mr Crane who's up there. And I wouldn't blame her. He seems all right. And they say what he doesn't know about paintings and all that antiquey sort of stuff you could get into a pill box. I'll tell you this, too. When he wants to he can knock back a pint of bitter with the best.'

16

'How do you know?'

'Because I met him in the White Horse at Exford one lunchtime. He was over there making sketches of some of the horses. Wizard they were. Just a few lines and it was all there. What's he doing at the Swales' anyway?'

'I dunno. Something for Sir Anthony and all his pictures and antiques and things. He's got a great big cellar kind of place. Runs all the way almost under the house . . . you know, with special heating and ventilators to keep things right. There's crates of things down there, too, that's never been unpacked.'

'She's a fair bit younger than Sir Anthony, isn't she?'

'Yes . . . '

He looked at her sideways briefly and then said, 'They don't get on all that good, people say.'

'Not all that good. But that's no business of yours or mine.'

'You reckon this chap Crane's got anything going with her? You know . . . when the cat's away the mice will play and she's a fine piece of — '

She smacked his face with something less than the full force she could have used and then got out of the car. As he followed and began to lift her bicycle down, knowing that

17

there was no hope of driving her up to the Swale house now, he said contritely, 'Sorry, Marge.'

'I don't like people who talk dirty of others without cause. How would you feel if you heard a chap in a pub say something like that about us?'

'I'd tear his head off.'

'I wonder? I think you're just a big talker.'

She took the bicycle from him and rode away without a backward glance. As she went there slowly grew a pleasant smile of satisfaction on her face. Some chaps, she told herself, were all right — just so long as you kept them in their place. And, of course, it was nice to have a proper chance of putting a man down — especially if you were really fond of him and . . . well . . . probably in time would be his wife. After all, there were some things you just couldn't do once you were married . . . at least, not without upsetting the whole apple cart.

She cycled up the long drive of pleached limes, the new leaf moving slightly in the faint breeze, the sunlight enamelling their colour. The tubbed young bay trees had been brought out of the conservatory and now sat spaced like green exclamation marks along the gravelled veranda. Across the front of the house's long Palladian façade the massive and ancient growth of wisteria was full of near-to-blooming racemes.

She cycled round to the back of the house into the cobbled stable yard and the two fox terriers gave her an obligatory barking welcome, moving from mock fierceness to fawning pleasure at seeing her again.

In the big kitchen she found the long table laid out with silver which awaited her cleaning. It was the cook's and the house-maid's afternoon off and the housekeeper would be in her room, feet up on her bed and lost in the high excitement of some, she told herself, sloppy old book of romance where girls fainted and blushed and shivered and trembled and lived between the heaven of bliss and the black cave of despair. Well, that was all right for some . . . but just now and again if a chap got too stroppy there was nothing for it except a smart backhander . . . unless, of course, you knew at the back of your mind that you were dealing with Mr Right. And as far as that went she wasn't a hundred per cent sure that Steve Black was Mr Right . . .

After she had been working for just over half an hour, the door opened and Lady Swale came in. As Margery began to rise to her feet, saying, 'Good afternoon, ma'am . . .' Lady Swale motioned her to sit down and said, 'How are you, Margery?'

'Very well, thank you, ma'am.'

'That's good. And the family?'

Margery smiled. 'Well, Ma's back's playing her up and Dad says the hay harvest won't be so good this year. But he says that every year. We lost a few Spring lambs with that late snow. But there . . . Nothing ever goes right all the way round, does it, ma'am?'

Daphne Swale smiled, slipped the index finger of her right hand under a stray lock of her blonde hair and tidied it, and said, 'Maybe not. But perhaps we shouldn't like it if it did. Nothing to worry about — wouldn't you miss that?'

'I don't know, ma'am. But I wouldn't mind giving it a try.'

'Will you tell your father that Sir Anthony's coming down today and will be over sometime to see him about the fencing of the Top Wood pasture. I should think it would be after lunch some time.'

'Yes, ma'am, I'll do that.'

Lady Swale eyed her for a moment or two and then smiling said, 'You've got your hair styled differently. I like it.'

'Thank you, ma'am.'

With Lady Swale gone Margery sat for a moment or two, idle, thinking about her. There were all sorts of stories going the rounds. Not that anything wrong was said about her — except perhaps that she should have more spirit and stand up to Sir Anthony. Put him in his place. Though, given what he was, that would never be easy. It was bad enough with her father's bit of land that marched with some of Sir Anthony's . . . neither of them gave an inch over who did this or that . . . or at least not right away and then one day they would meet somewhere along the brook — they fought over that, too, about the fishing rights and the bed clearance and the flood baulks to stop bank erosion — and suddenly, like the sun breaking through grey clouds, they would be all smiles.

She could hear her father now saying, 'He's a wicked bugger, you know. 'Course, with all his money he can afford to be. Mind you — he don't squander it — that house and his place never lacks for a thing, and they do tell me he's got lovely pictures and stuff up there worth fortunes. I know'd him once when he was a-talking down by the cattle grid, top end of his drive, and he was arguing and so was I about whether he did something or I did something over some fencing and then one of them . . . what you call peacock butterflies comes and perches right on his hand where it rested on a post top. And he looked at it and said, 'There's a hell of a lot in this world that

21

men can do — but never anything as lovely as this beauty could he make . . . Oh, he can come some way towards it. I could show you things to prove it. But the great craftsman was, is, and ever will be, God above.' Aye, that's what he said, and him as big a lecher as any, tighter fisted than most, and — God forgive me for saying it, since it's only my guess — more wicked than anyone could imagine.'

Many people wondered how much of all the tales told about Sir Anthony were true. There certainly were enough to pick from. His great-grandfather had been a South Wales coalmine-owner, a man born into riches and dedicated to dying far wealthier than the day he had been born. In retirement he had crossed the Bristol Channel from Swansea, bought land above the brook and built himself a fine house of little architectural interest but with grounds of great beauty — for with retirement he had discovered an untapped talent for landscape gardening and had been delighted that his hands, so long turning all he touched into money, now freed from that coarse employ, were the hands of a true gardener, so that, although he employed in the early days of the garden's creation nearly a score of men, he worked happily with them in the planting of shrubs and trees and the creation of formal, wild and water gardens and the great ride of still far from mature yews which flanked the driveway to the house. After him came son, grandson and then a great-grandson — the present Sir Anthony Swale, Bart. — who saw to it that the gardens and estate were kept in the same immaculate state as in his great-grandfather's days. But with the present baronet the passion for fine gardens, terraces and ornamental lakes was not of the same intensity as that of the old mine-owner. But he too nourished his own passions, and had the wealth to indulge them. He smoked and drank too much, and then at times forced abstinence on himself almost as though finding pleasure in self-flagellation. Although part of his nature was coarse, ruthless and libertine he was also consumed with a love of beauty and a lust for acquiring paintings, sculptures, rare books and antique jewellery.

When he wanted something the lust in him, although almost always controlled and schooled, burned at white heat until he could turn desire into possession. Women, too, raised something of the same desire in him, and when he wanted one he would take imperiously if he sensed this was to be the true road to possession, or he would buy if the pleasure was, no matter how delicately indicated, available at a market price.

Only once had he been near complete frustration and that was with his wife, Daphne — the only daughter of a then widowed Professor of Divinity at Oxford. But in the end, after a year of wearing false colours modestly and conducting himself while with father or daughter with a probity which he assumed as though — and indeed almost felt it to be — it were a hair shirt, he overcame the father's weak suspicions on his daughter's behalf and married Daphne.

Within three years he had had to admit that for once he had been drawn into a bad bargain . . . bad from his point of view. He had thought that he had it in his power to turn a sheltered, inexperienced Churchman's daughter into a passionate, willing, entirely obedient bedmate. But between them, from his first tentative demands to his later brusque, near brutal, assertions of his marital — and bizarrely erotic — rights there had never once flowered for her any abandonment of mind and body in the meeting of their flesh or their temperaments. In one way only did they come near meeting. They both loved man-made beauty — she, the garden his great-grandfather had created and also some of the paintings and fine china and jewellery he collected. There were times when she

24

wondered even with his inherited and own-made wealth that he could afford his mania — but, in a rare good mood, once he told her that she need never have cause to worry about that. He had money all over the world, and there were few countries that would be loath to give him hospitality. And he had used a favourite phrase of his to dismiss the whole subject — *It's a bad way to live looking too far ahead. Watch the ground just in front of your feet.*

★ ★ ★

Richard Crane, sitting on an unopened crate, smoking the fifth of the ten cigarettes he allowed himself during a day, heard the whine of the descending house lift and knew that it would be Lady Swale . . . the title, as always when he thought of her, helping him to establish a little more distance between them, since he knew his own feelings towards her. It was not often that she came down these days. When he had started work for Sir Anthony Swale a year ago she had used to come down a lot . . . but then the thing had happened and they had both with unspoken prudence made their own declaration and put into action their shared denial of any future for the feeling each had raised in the other.

He was over forty and, for all his expertise, knew that he was going nowhere, too lost in his love and worship of man's works. Envy was the ever-present element in all his passions . . . envy of Sir Anthony's great collection which he was cataloguing and envy of the man's possessing Daphne Swale. Those two elements held him almost complacently prisoner at Swale Place.

For just a few seconds nearly a year ago he had without thought followed his body's instinct and put his arms around her and, without surprise, had known hers around him and their lips meeting and their bodies close held in one another's embrace. No more than that. No words when the embrace was broken. No words needed. Sir Anthony was his employer — a good one — and her husband — a bad one. But for them, no matter what their own emotions, there was no future together. When they had stepped apart she had gone to the tea-tray she had brought down and poured a cup for him. When she had turned to present it to him, she had smiled faintly and just shaken her head as she sighed, the deep drawing in and out of breath a sadness of sound which still haunted his memory most days.

He went over to the lift and opened its half-glass-fronted door.

He said, 'You're early.'

'I know. I wanted to get the cottage key from you. I've bought some stuff for new bedroom curtains. I want to take the measurements.'

'I see. Well, that's lovely.' He fished in his pocket and handed her the key. 'New curtains. Nice surprise. What are they like?'

'Oh, tropical birds and flowers. I didn't think you wanted Spring lambs and primrose banks.'

'Sounds lovely. Sir Anthony's coming down today, isn't he?'

'Later, yes.'

He smiled. 'Or sooner. You never know with him. Not about time. Or about art. He's the most extraordinary man for a collector I've ever met. I've unpacked and catalogued about a half of the stuff down here. Jewellery, paintings, a few small bronzes . . . all French, Italian, Spanish stuff. But today I opened a new crate — and out comes that.' He nodded to an icon which he had set up against a chair. It showed the figure of a haloed saint, seated and holding a sword across his knees while to the left of the figure an angel flew towards the saint bearing a crown in her hands.

'What is it?'

'It's a Russian icon. Actually it's an icon of

27

Saint Demetrius of Salonika. It's probably early thirteenth century. He's supposedly the patron saint of soldiers. I've seen one a bit like it before in the Tretiakov Gallery in Moscow. It's the first Russian thing I've come across. Did Sir Anthony ever go there?'

'I wouldn't know.' She smiled. 'He doesn't tell me much about his travels . . . all business, he says, and boring.'

'I must ask him how he got it. Probably it was smuggled out. It happens.'

'If it was something he saw and wanted — then he'd find ways of getting it.'

Crane shook his head. 'He's an extraordinary man. I've never seen such stuff. And he doesn't seem to have followed any line. Paintings, jewellery, books . . . a few good modern things, I mean twenties art nouveau — and then, bingo! I find a dog-eared sketch book full of Picasso drawings that must be worth a bomb. You know, there are times when I think I'm not really the man to bring any sort of order to it all. He should have three or four people on this job. Just under a year I've been here and I haven't really scratched the surface . . . There's a cabinet up the far end and it's full of old cigarette cards. Famous footballers and cricketers. Famous actresses and British birds. And three marvellous sets of lead soldiers . . . one of

28

them all Boer War regiments and leaping, spear-shaking Zulus . . . But they wouldn't be Boer War, would they? No. Zulu War. Don't know much about that. I tell you, I did four years with Sotheby's Fine Arts . . . but this lot! Aladdin's Cave. That's what it must be. Aladdin's Cave.'

She said, 'I'm sure you're the man for the job. Sir Anthony never makes mistakes when he employs people. Or, if he does, he finds out quickly and they go in far shorter time than just under a year.'

Crane grinned. 'I shall grow old and grey-bearded down here. But — ' he looked her full in the eyes, ' — there are compensations for living like a troglodyte most of the day.'

To his surprise, knowing he had deliberately overstepped the mark a little, he saw a smile pass quickly over her face and then she gently shook her head at him and turned away towards the lift.

In his cottage, which lay off the main drive at the foot of the falling ground which held a great sweep of rhododendron bushes, some of them already in full bloom, she took down the old sitting room curtains and hung the new ones. He kept the whole place neat and tidy . . . in fact, she thought, if anything he was excessively tidy in his own appearance and about the cottage. She went upstairs, not to make his bed or tidy his room — both tasks would already have been done by him — but to take the measurements for new curtains.

Her days were long and more and more she found a quiet peace of mind in working with her hands . . . embroidery, new curtains, a simple dress for herself. With such work her mind seemed to be released into a new freedom of imagination . . . she saw herself in a hundred different guises and forms . . . always a woman, always herself, but with the world around her completely obedient to her shaping and its people strictly under her control. A world, she knew, created deliberately for her own pleasure.

Both she and her husband, sharing the same want, had been assured after clinical tests that there was no impediment in either to deny natural conception. Yet none resulted and she had long ago shaped for herself the comforting figment of a dream child . . . now son, now daughter . . . a fantasy which held comfort, short-lived, but needed to sustain her and keep at bay the slow distress that overbore her at times. And, too, she had the grace and honesty to recognize that with her husband there was much of the same feeling. He had a younger brother, long dead, whose son was his heir. This nephew, now a Church of England priest, a family man, he had long ago come to accept as his heir. But it had taken time — harrowing time for her.

Possession was his passion. Great house, wide lands, money, fine works of art, high friends, and wanton and willing women of high class and good family. He had a lust for the best. But the gods had denied him — despite the assurances of all specialists that gynaecologically there was no impediment — the one thing he wanted, a son to carry his name and to grow into man's estate and to ride the broad acres and sit at the long boardroom tables in his place one day. When that need, desire, passion . . . almost mania . . . sometimes overrode him in rare moments there was no predicting the run his mood would take.

Once, he had lain in her arms and sobbed like a denied child. Another time he had railed against her, accusing her of taking anti-conception pills, potions . . . God knows what . . . all to pleasure herself at his frustration. At such times she feared him greatly — because it was then that his mania made him a stranger to her, and at rare intervals he would beat her . . . but — and she could think this cynically, although she had a great compassion for him — never in

31

any way to mar her daytime appearance.

Staring out of the cottage bedroom window now, a robust Spring wind ruffling the long swathes of blooming daffodils under the yews which lined the drive, she knew that for all her strength of spirit there must come a day when she could live with it no longer alone. In that moment she knew how it would be because imagination, long a great soothing element in her, had shown it to her. To some other woman she would suddenly find herself telling all . . . or, and even now she rebuked herself with the thought, circumstance would trap her as it might today if Richard Crane were to return to the cottage unexpectedly and climb the stairs to find her here . . . and, in her remote fantasy, not even he, but any man thrown up by time and chance and with the simple gift of kind words and a loving touch. Fantasy, too, sustained her with the wildest — and she felt, the wickedest of hopes. His business took him all over the world . . . a plane crash. He rode to hounds like a demon, possessed. He drove his car on the motorways with a cold, searing, passion for speed . . . perhaps, she had sometimes thought, for oblivion. Only rarely now did he turn true lover, gentle and kind, thoughtful, and warm with affection and openly grieving at his past behaviour.

She turned from the window and, moving to the door, stopped for a moment to straighten the coverlet of the hastily, man-made bed. A book of verse lay on the bedside table with an old envelope for marker half protruding from its page tops. She opened it and her eyes were taken at once, with some shock at such usage, by the under-scoring of a few lines which read:

> . . . What I do
> And what I dream include thee, as
> the wine
> Must taste of its own grapes. And
> when I sue
> God for myself, He hears that name
> of thine,
> And sees within my eyes the tears of
> two.

She went down and walked back up the drive, thinking to herself that Crane lived in a world of beauty . . . paintings, fine sculptures. He was likeable, and she, out of her own loneliness, could admit frankly that he was the kind of man she might fall in love with easily. At this moment, though, there was no one she loved. Even the love of God was at times conventional . . . unreal for most of the week and then awakening and shaming her at worship on Sundays. She remembered her father saying, 'It's easy for people only in want turning to God. But that's only putting your snout into the Sunday pig-trough. If only an empty belly or a worried conscience turns you to God then what more can you expect than a dusty answer?'

At the moment she was suddenly aware that the bird song from the shrubberies and the gardens had suddenly stopped. The unexpected silence made her look around as though somewhere near she would find the cause for the birds' silence. Seeing nothing she looked up and then saw, so high above her against the afternoon sun glare in the sky that she could not be sure of her eyes, the slow glide across the far blue of the dark crescent of a peregrine falcon. She had seen such birds before, but seldom over the estate. Two years previously while walking in the top plantation with her husband she had seen one come beating over the wooded crest against a stiff wind and her husband, seeing it also for his eyes missed little, had said with a grin, 'If I could lay my hands on a young falcon ... perhaps a brace ... I know an oil sheik who would call me brother and put more business my way than I could handle ...'

* * *

34

As Sir Anthony Swale's wife walked up the yew avenue to her house, about one hundred miles to the east Sir John Warboys, K.B.E., pulled up just beyond a Hampshire river bridge under a horse chestnut tree slowly moving into full and flaming red blossom. With the engine switched off there came to him the incessant, bullying calling of a chiff-chaff and, high above it, the fading challenge of a lark's aspiring song. God, he told himself with an old man's easiness of mind, was in His Heaven and the lay-by bins were full and long over-spilling with human rubbish, and the young hawthorns in the hedge bank were colourful with a crop of blue and red windblown potato crisp bags. God's good growth and man's wanton waste and the human eye, he thought, now so used to the mixture that for the most part it went unmarked. Near seventy years had left him now without any strong emotions to be stirred by the eyes' affront. Lacking the slightest sense of irreverence — for he was old and tired and gave more than mere lip service to his faith despite a career too full of obligatory sinning on his country's behalf — he wondered how much longer it would be before He grew tired of human antics, then, bored with *homo sapiens* and all his known dirty tricks and selfish predictabilities, might give Himself the relief of turning it all into a completely different video game . . . Aye, maybe named Armageddon.

Smiling to himself at the conceit, he got out of the car and walked back to the river bridge and looked over. The water was colouring down to a rare bluey-greenness that followed heavy rain. A little way downstream, rod in hand and wadered, was Dicky Quint, another retired servant of the Queen and justly rewarded by being made a Knight of the British Empire. He looked up and gave a wave of his hand and then went on with his fishing, working his way upstream to the bridge without success. When he reached it he anchored his dry fly in the soft cork of the rod's butt. Looking up he said, 'I wasn't expecting you until dinner time.'

'Nice surprise?'

'I hope it is, but I doubt it. Whenever did you leave London purely for pleasure?'

'Many a time, but always incognito.'

'You're not wearing an official hat any longer. So, you can expect nothing from me.'

'Not even curiosity?'

'I hung that up with my official hat.'

'That could never be. Even now you are going over the probabilities and chances of varying alternatives. What is the future about to offer . . . ? Yes?'

Quint grinned and quoted, ''Heaven from all creatures hides the book of Fate — ''

''All but the page prescribed, their present state.''

Quint said, 'I say he comes before not after Shakespeare.'

'Never, my dear Quint. Who would put a Pope before God?'

Quint laughed and waved him away. Warboys went back to his car. It had been a nice moment or two of their old form of banter. Memory seldom failed them. Whenever they needed them the ghosts of human shapes and the silent run of the written words of the great surfaced. Half an hour later Quint joined him, took down his rod and got into the car. As they drove off to cover the short distance to his house he said, 'Whatever it is — I don't want to hear about it until after dinner. I've known you too long not to know the seasons of your face. So save it until the port.'

'Does it all show so plainly?'

'Aye, for one who knows how to read you. Also this is not the first time you have come wandering into my sylvan retreat to add more ghosts to my already over-haunted sleep. All I ask now is do I know, respect . . . aye, even love him or her?'

'Professional respect. No love. And *him* not *her.*'

'Aye, well then. That makes me a little more comfortable. But overall, given my life again, I would still take Government service . . . aye, but as a Civil Servant with my name, rank, and honours and annual salary free for all to read in Whitaker's Almanack, that fat little pony of a book cavorting so gaily around all those overworked, spavined cart horses of the *Encyclopedia Britannica* as they trudge from *A* to *Anno* and on through *Vase* to *Zygo.* I speak, of course, of the Nineteen Forty-Six edition . . . dear, dear — why have you come to drag me back even if only for a little while? No, no — don't tell me. Just give me a clue or so to brood on until we have dined and come to the port.'

'Art collector, world-wide business interests. Business in quotes in some cases. West countryman. Baronet and — '

'Say no more.' He sighed. 'Idiot . . . the gods gave him a paradise and the money to run it. What is it that gets into a man to make him take a course which can only in the end lead to his own destruction?'

'You know the answer to that. Every man considers himself the exception that disproves the rule. So many have tried and failed . . . with some the failure coming late, but nevertheless come it does. And so: I am here. Unofficially. Our meeting is not taking place. You are deep in dreaming sleep. What sadness, what sadness . . . you give a man the world and he wants more. When the table groans with good victuals, and the wine jugs are full, no sane man spoils the feast by teasing himself with the grim fantasy of future hunger and thirst. Or — and far worse — for all he has in possessions and passions fair and virtuous some demon is roused in him to seek more . . . to know that only glut and gluttony are the true staples of existence.'

Quint sighed. 'Why cannot we be left alone? Our time has been served.'

'Only when our time runs out do we cease to be on call. Ours was the Devil's ordination. Anyway — this is a simple matter. I have a list of names we can go through over some of your excellent port. But there should be no difficulty in selecting a man. No genius is called for — and little finesse.'

Quint laughed dryly. 'A common type. The kind for whom the gods unaccountably often have a soft spot. Beneath the river bridge back along there used to be a fat three-pounder trout that spurned all my guile and so beguilingly tied flies. Two weeks ago, as I watched from the bridge before fishing, a village lad landed it using a fly that was a misshapen mess of floss and feather. So do the gods reward the unregarding. So, Sir Anthony is to go. There is no child, no son to follow. The widow grieves. For how long I wonder . . . ? *Weep no more, lady, weep no more . . .* and so on . . . *for violets plucked the sweetest showers — Will ne'er make grow again.* And will a friar of orders grey walk behind his cortège a-telling of his beads?'

'Of a certainty — there is no man in the world at whose death there cannot be found one true sorrower. God's mercy sees to that.' Then after a little silence Warboys went on, 'It comes to me now that perhaps little Alfie Grey would be our man . . . However, we can leave all that until later.'

★ ★ ★

The falcon flew westwards towards far Countisbury Point. He was a mile offshore and lazed his way, yet now and then, as though to ease the growing fever in his blood, he turned over and dropped towards some seabird winging the wave tops below him. But always long before he reached the gull or tern he would swing up and let his momentum take him skywards until the drag of the sea-pull finally held him and then he would half roll to level flight and with lazy wing beats move westwards. Before him was the long stretch of the distant horizon broken by the cliffs of Lundy Island's eastern shore. He flew over Countisbury Point, gaining height now all the while, saw one of his own kind and sex far below him and knew through flesh and feather that there lay no welcome of the kind he sought . . . of the kind that made him suddenly stoop at a black-headed gull only to swing up within two feet of the seabird and let the force of his own momentum take him skyward until it died and so with a half roll he came to even keel and flew on. Beyond Ilfracombe and Bull Point he winged for a while south towards Barnstaple Bay and the mouths of the Taw and the Torridge rivers but some vagrant impulse turned him away and he climbed a few hundred feet and, clearer now to the west, saw the white churning of breakers around the near shore of Lundy Island.

He idled there on a gentle following wind, the long strip of the island lengthening as he approached it, its eastern shores alive with the movement of seabirds. He came in over Tibbett's Point and swung north, following the coastline and leaving behind him a quietness of seabird call and movement. Off North-East Point he stooped with no more than playful intent at a wave-crest flying cormorant, saw the bird crash on the sea's surface and then dive and stay clear in his sight as it swung shorewards. He beat up two hundred feet and in a short while was high over Seals' Rock and rounding the North-West Point of the island. There it was, where the island's highest cliffs faced the open Atlantic and the long run of its great seas, where the rock faces were alive with colonies of razorbills, guillemots, shags and gulls, that his nameless drive was quietened: for from a high ledge south of the Point she came out and beat slowly upwards, leaving behind her on the ledge whitened with sea-bird droppings the empty feathered frame of her tiercel mate who from Spring health and vigour had sickened and wasted its way to death from the shotgun blast of an ignorant and too hasty youth as it had risen from a small bird kill in the thick heather before him. None of this on the island — but on the mainland to the south. But with the last of its strength it had turned north to find its mate and birthplace.

He climbed above her, mewed, and then dropped, wings half-closed, and swung away across the top of the cliffs and the heath and sheep-bitten grass to the far side of the island. She followed him but when he held directly eastwards over the remains of the old Battery and, with the sea under him, began to make height with sharp, clipping wings she turned back.

Four times he came back after her refusals to follow him, and four times from high pitch he dived and raked the air within inches of her head as he passed. But on the fifth time as he came to her she turned below him in a tight circle and from the top of her loop straightened into following flight after him eastward over the heaving waters.

That night they roosted on a rock ledge, thirty feet above high-water mark at the foot of Hurlstone Point. At dawn he left her and took a mallard duck in the water meadow where the Aller brook ran to the pebble ridge. He brought it back to her on the rock ledge and shuffled away, bobbing and swaying his head, until she came to the mating gift and began to tear at the soft down and breast feathers to come to the good meat. Twice that day he trod her. And of all the people — no great number — who used the cliff path that day, only one person marked the pair, and that by pure accident. Walking up to her usual resting place, the National Trust seat, Mrs Winslade saw the tiercel come low, flying down the combe from Bossington Hill. It passed within fifty yards of her where she sat motionless, dipped towards the sea and called. As it did so she saw something drop from one of its claws . . . a small bird, lark or pipit . . . and as it tumbled through the air the female falcon winged out from her cliff ledge and took the offering as it came to her with a half-roll and the sweep of a taloned foot. Both birds then flew low over the sea and disappeared around the point.

Mrs Winslade said nothing of her sighting to anyone.

2

At six o'clock that evening, as in far East
Hampshire Quint and Warboys were finishing
their early whiskies before going up to their
rooms to change for dinner, the Westland
helicopter came low over the valley ridge,
circled widely over the domain once, as
though Sir Anthony Swale wished to assure
himself that all was as it had been when he
had left his home and estate, and then settled
with a noisy clattering and a grass-flattening
squall of air currents in the small paddock
adjacent to the cottage where Richard Crane
lodged and where Crane himself now stood at
his garden fence watching the machine land.

He saw Sir Anthony get out of the
machine, turn and say something to the pilot
and then, briefcase in hand, walk away and
from a safe distance halt and watch the
machine take off, gain altitude quickly, and
finally disappear over the eastward ridge of
the valley.

Richard Crane met him at the paddock
gate, holding it open as a matter of courtesy
to his employer and wondering why — knowing all that he did about this fair-haired,

high-cheekboned man, with his easy charm and grand passion for works of art — he liked him so much.

'Evening, Richard.' It had been 'Crane' for some months at first and then, his loyalty and expertise apparent and his manner pleasant, even amusing at times, the Christian name had been awarded like a well-deserved accolade.

'Evening, Sir Anthony. Good trip?'

'Only from Bristol. Left the car there. How's everything?'

'Oh, fine. Always something new, too.' He grinned. After all these months he still could not make up his mind whether he liked or disliked this man. He was, it seemed, always lagging behind the sharp changes of the baronet's moods. 'Did you know . . . and I would swear on oath to their authenticity . . . that you had a case of gold enamelled hat medallions, most of them set with sapphires? There's a beautiful one of St George and the Dragon . . . It must be, I think, early seventeenth century and probably Hungarian or Bohemian?'

'I seem to recall it.'

Sir Anthony looked with a smile at Crane. He could give him a few years in age, liked him, and respected his knowledge and enthusiasm. For a moment or two he

46

thought, easily containing his private and long-habituated anguish, how refreshing and heart and soul-easing it would be to have this man's simple joy in things of beauty and, above that, the connoisseur's expertise to look beyond beauty to its provenance and creation. A lovely woman, or desirable woman, was a woman, a thing of want or lust whom one took by whatever guile or bribe to which experience so surely prompted one — but once taken . . . well, *post coitum omne animal triste* . . . But if a man had a Botticelli on his wall . . . God knows anything as rare as the *Birth of Venus* was a million light years out of his reach . . . there could never be any *tristitia*. The smile still lighting his finely boned face, he said, 'You're doing a good job for me. And when it's finished you shall be well rewarded. And I tell you this — true love is, I think, the provenance of much evil. Why? Because in its name there are no crimes or betrayals in this world which have not been committed.'

Richard Crane laughed. 'My father warned me against becoming a stockbroker or banker — he had been both in his time — and put me in the way of the fine arts knowing that he would leave me enough money to live by beauty and never lack for a good breakfast. But he knew nothing of lust — true lust which is fiercer and stronger than true love. Men kill and most wars are fought from a lust for power, for land . . . or, aye, if you like, for Helen of Troy — so they think. But I fancy that truly men fight, and men are drawn to evil ways, because most of us are yet still far from redemption. It's easier to sin than to accept the strictures of virtue.'

Sir Anthony laughed. 'Good Lord — you should say it all from the church pulpit next Sunday and all our friends shall be invited.'

'No, thank you, sir.'

'Well, perhaps not. Anyway, I'll see you tomorrow morning.'

Daphne Swale had heard and seen the helicopter from her bedroom window. She was about to bath and change before dinner. There had been a telephone message from him that morning that he was coming — but alone, no guests. That he would come she knew — but that he might at the last moment bring guest or guests was far from an improbability. Holding her bathrobe about her, she watched the drive and eventually saw him turn into it, fair hair awry in the growing evening breeze, a briefcase swinging in his right hand. He walked with the swing and easy carriage of a young man and, in the distance, it was easy for her to create the young man she had married and by whom she had been tamed and trained to his ways. But tamed only, she knew, in body — her own spirit and personality she kept free so that even in the ambiguities of his lovemaking she could regard herself as a stranger watching a stranger performing those acts which, had they been evoked by true love's passion, would have been as normal and acceptable as a breakfast table smile, the reaching out of a hand as one walked some dusking moments in the rock garden to caress and with joy share the run of her buttocks and the slow rhythm of a moving hip, and giving and taking of passion's wandering and adventuring kisses and caresses as they lay abed. Not what is done or wanted she thought to herself but the barrenness of legal rape and debauchery which, she guessed, so many wives endured.

Instinct and observation told her that it would be so now. She had seen him talking and laughing with Richard Crane. She saw him now, briefcase swinging as a boy would swing his satchel in the freedom of leaving school.

He came into the room, closed the door, and stood smiling at her and then, after drawing in a deep breath, let it go free as though he were collapsing with the strain of high tension. He said, 'My God — you look bloody marvellous . . . '

He came to her, his hands taking the revers of her dressing robe and sliding it downwards to reveal her breasts and body. He lifted her and laid her on the bed and turned his back to her as he undressed. When he came to her he was, as sometimes rarely he could be, gentle and almost supplicatingly passionate, begging with mute caresses for the licence he needed and which she granted him knowing that, even if momentarily denied, it would turn him from wooing to near rape. He used her gently and she thought that with love, true love and true devotion, she could have given him all he asked with joy and shared ecstasy — but the time for that had passed years ago. They lay and talked for a while afterwards and then he went to his rooms to shave and bath.

Mrs Winslade was coming to dinner. She was far from his favourite person but this evening he felt tolerant and easy-going. He shaved, bathed and dressed and then went down to the long underground gallery which he had made by converting most of the house's cellars.

On a small desk he found Crane's ledgers with their lists of his acquisitions. He sat down and lit a cigarette, coughed gently against the first strong inhaling of its smoke, and then opened the ledger at random. As he ran his eye over the pages he felt his shoulders tense with satisfaction. Most of his collection he had bought with his own money. But some objects he could never have acquired legitimately . . . and never would have done, except for a chance meeting on a Swedish island beach. God knew how many years ago . . . but she had shown him the way, trapping him first with her beauty and body into a near-besotted state of constant desire. But more than that, by showing him things which raised a rarer lust in him for possession. As if to convenience him — his father had died early and there was none to say nay or question his wants or desires. Except . . . good humoured now, he could shrug his shoulders indulgently . . . his wife, who still shared his bed though never these days with another woman on the far side of him . . . never ever, in fact, more than four or five times until one day some now almost forgotten highborn baggage had said, 'Tony — don't do it. Don't push her. If you do . . . she's the quiet kind who could do anything.' So he had taken the good advice.

Lying in a shallow tray on a bed of cotton wool was a beautifully coloured piece of glasswork of the Madonna and Child and two supporting saints. A card in

Crane's handwriting read — *Mid-eighteenth-century Italian (Murano). There is an almost identical piece in the Museo Vetrario, Murano.*

For a moment or two there was a touch of envy in him at the man's knowledge. Against his patchwork knowledge, the other was a walking encyclopaedia of arts and antiquities. Nice chap, quiet, well-mannered, and no weakling — he was a tiger on the tennis court . . . and what else? A quiet one. Like his own wife. Maybe they had already come together to ease their solitude? No, couldn't think so. He would have known since there was always something that gave the inexperienced away. The experienced didn't care a damn any way.

The intercom speaker clicked and his wife's voice said, 'Tony — Mrs Winslade's car's coming up the drive. Will you come and do the drinks?'

He picked up the speaker on the desk and said, 'Okay — I'll come and look after the old bag.'

Going to the lift door, his hand on the light switch, he took a last look around. Three quarters of the stuff here either he or his father before him had acquired with their own money. But there was a lot, much of it still crated, which he could not have laid his hands on except for that meeting, still golden in his memory, with the blonde Venus who would have delighted Botticelli. How easily he had been trapped . . . but only because deep in his heart he had known the unimportance of life unless it held moments of rashness and high danger. Life without these would have lacked savour and his wild spirit slowly unmanned . . . With Drake he could have sailed for Eldorado. But now the risks which shadowed him were no more than the uncertainty of the seas Drake had ridden.

The intercom said, 'Tony, darling, Mrs Winslade's here.'

He switched off the gallery lights and went to the lift, and the odd thought struck him that there were a few around these parts who still wondered whether Mr Winslade had been pushed or slipped. Hell hath no fury . . .

★ ★ ★

The light going fast, so that he could no longer garden, Alfie Grey came into the scullery, eased off his gumboots and slid his feet into the tartan-pattern slippers which were obligatory wear in the parlour — unless they had guests and then he wore his church-going highly polished black boots. Going to wash his hands, neck and face in the sink he said, 'I thought I heard the phone thing go?'

'That's right.' His wife came in from the parlour and began to set the kitchen table. 'I stewed up the cold lamb for supper, some nice new potatoes and carrots. And did you fancy just cheese after or what's left of the cold bread pudding?'

'I'll have both, but the cold bread pudding first. I thought I heard the telephone.'

'That's right. You did.'

'Who was it?'

She stood in front of him, a tall gaunt woman whom he had married as a tall, gaunt girl of twenty-five, not from love but from beer which had made him amorous so that he had, for the first time in his life, been carried away by emotion — on a dark night of fumbling and panting in the back of his delivery van . . . well, not his, but the one he drove for the laundry which, after late deliveries, he used to park outside her house. During his four years in the Army he had fallen in love again and forever. Firearms had seduced him . . . from his first awkward fumbling with a new recruit's nervousness with a Lee Enfield .303 . . . then right through the desert chasing Rommel and up through Italy as far as Monte Cassino where he got a leg wound from a wedged-shaped piece of hand grenade (Mills) clumsily de-pinned and dropped by one of his own comrades while, as Alfie described it — 'Assin' around, pissed to the world on *vino verde.*' The result was that six hours before rain came Alfie walked with a limp and a rather gay shrug of the shoulders which went well with the beaming and usually quite sincere smile on his face. *A happy smile wiles away many a weary mile.* He was a great walker, a highly knowledgeable collector of grasses, reeds and rushes, and as cold and calculating a killer as any with a mind to murder could wish to hire. However, he worked solely for the most respectable of clients. To anyone curious about his way of work he said frankly he had none . . . not since the day his missus had come up on the pools and his own father had died and left him enough to see him by.

'That gentleman of yours.'

'Oh, him.'

'Said would you call him. The number's on the pad. You think this means he'll want you to go off all over the place again?'

'Could be.'

'Then I shall go to Milly's place. She's always on for me to go over there. That'll make a nice break for both of us. He said to phone around ten o'clock tonight. I writ the

55

number down on the pad.'

'Ta . . .'

He went on with his washing and then as he towelled hands and face dry he thought, not able to deny the birth of pleasure in him, that it had been two years since the last one — and that had been a very quick one. What he liked most was a real teaser. Sitters were too easy. It was all scientific really. Study your man, learn his habits and his timetables . . . Sometimes his gentleman left it all to him. *Just drop him at your first chance* . . . and another time . . . well there'd be a string of things that had to be right first. In a way it was a kind of science — and no question of conscience 'cause his gentleman had sworn on oath that they was all enemies of Her Majesty the Queen.

Long may she reign over us . . . God save the Queen.

He wondered what they would give him? Sometimes they let him use one of his own. Another time, no. Sometimes it was something modern and other times and for no reason he would ever know — nor have the impudence to ask — it would be unusual — like last time it was a .404 Magazine rifle, a Cogswell and Harrison, taking a 400 grain bullet with an energy of over four thousand feet-pounds which could knock down the toughest big game . . . like an elephant or rhino — or some dirty foreign bastard what was a thorn in the side of the Queen's peace. Yes . . . he'd liked that one . . . a special three-shot alloy magazine and one cartridge in the chamber — making four in all. And enough. When had he ever had to use more than one? Five times over twice that many years? Not a bad record. And the money was too good to turn down . . . Also if it was a good area he might pick up some new grasses for his collection . . . he was still missing a few sedges. Maybe it could be Scotland . . . Sutherland (what a hope!) where he might get the elusive *Carex chordorrhiza* — if he didn't get himself pulled under in a bog.

Coming to the table and sitting down, waiting to be served, he said, 'Some bugger's broke into Tom Colway's allotment shed and pinched all his tools. Know what I'd do with that type? String 'em up by the goolies — that 'ud learn 'em to respect other people's gear.'

His wife said sharply, 'Enough of that Alfie. It's all right when it's just the two of us — but one day you'm goin' to forget and say it with others here.'

'Not me.'

★ ★ ★

Dinner was over, and coffee already taken with liqueurs . . . the two women's glasses were now empty and gentle refusals had been made to the offer of more — such restraint he felt perhaps in general endemic with women. Over-indulgence was a primitive male instinct. Eat and drink now to the full — the next week's hunting may be barren of kills.

Looking at Mrs Winslade and re-creating something of the young girl she had once been, vaguely wondering in his mind whether her husband had slipped or been pushed, both possibilities with a drunken sot, he answered the question which she had put to him, 'I don't know. My father had it to some extent. He passed it on to me and, I suppose, you could say it has become near mania which after all is a polite way of saying madness. But I like to think of it in another way and that is a rage to own and preserve beauty . . . the beauty produced by man's genius and through which, if you wish, you can say he is God-touched, God-favoured. After all — the Church has long recognized this. It has always been the most ardent and consistent defender and harbourer of the *beaux arts*. Don't you agree?'

After a moment's thought Mrs Winslade said, 'Yes, I do. But the need for these acquisitions can lead surely to the opposite of what you call God-touched. No?'

He laughed. 'Why, of course. Already the Devil has all the best tunes. You don't think he would stop there? No, no . . . his agents are always busy, finding and buying for him — and he doesn't mind if his canvases or marbles last all eternity or are smashed or pulverized in a month or a moment . . . like Hiroshima. There's always more to come.'

'And your pleasure?'

'Simple. Of the eye and the mind's delight, and a genuine desire, when all has been catalogued and sorted, to give it away to the nation and hope that no one will think it egotistical that I should want it known as the Swale Bequest. Just that. A not immodest wish, you think?'

'I think it's a splendid idea.'

And so she did, but there was little surprise in her for years ago she had known this same disturbing set of contradictions in her own husband . . . so much good and so much bad. Oh, what a creature was man . . .

'I'm told that some of the things you've got are very rare . . . some unique. You must spend a lot of time looking for such things and perhaps even persuading their owners to sell. I know once my husband found in a cottage a lovely three-cornered wall cupboard which he knew I would love. But the old man who owned it wouldn't part with it at any price. You see it had been made by his great-grandfather and had been so much part of his life that it would have been like selling his great-grandfather.'

'I can understand that. Well, some day when Richard Crane has got a bit more forward with things I'll put some of it on exhibition. In any case it will all go to the nation in the fulness of time.'

After she had left and his own wife had gone up to bed, he sat with his last brandy, enjoying the thought of the future he was creating . . . and that, he hoped, a long-distant future when he would die full of years if not of good works. When the time was ripe he meant to make an arrangement with the Government that they would accept his collection in lieu of death duties.

After that it would be up to his nephew in his turn to protect and hold what would be his in whichever way he chose. Churchman he might be but he had a native shrewdness which he had schooled to run in harness with his Christian beliefs and duties.

He neither grumbled nor cared now about his own conscription on a Swedish island . . . damp sand on her naked breasts and buttocks and a flock of black-headed terns offshore feasting from a passing shoal of fish . . . and himself not long elected to Parliament . . . an up and coming number with everything ahead. Oh, yes, he had fallen but had not been foolish. He had driven the bargain hard. Sir Anthony Swale, Bart, as soon as his ailing father went. A safe constituency already his and the link man (a safe Churchman, God help us, who saw not Armageddon ahead but the Kingdom of Heaven on earth and the Russian bear lying down with the lamb) still living, now in his late seventies and still awaiting the Second Coming and occasionally taking a Confirmation service when a locum was needed in his parish church . . . a Bishop of course. Not only did the Devil get the best tunes but also quite a few of the best people.

He sat for a long time, drinking slowly and thinking. When he went up to bed he was coldly drunk and knew that if he lay by himself sleep would taunt him from a distance and the petty demons, who dared not mock and taunt him sober, would come and begin their torturing, mind-wounding inquisition. He undressed and went to his wife's room, cold with inner sobriety as the demons danced, his flesh proud, and his body and mind aching for the solace of taking what was his without leave or grace or tenderness

— weep though he might for himself the next morning in the solitude of his own room.

She was awake and, although she had no love for him, she understood. And no words passed between them. He used her and went and when she knew that he must be soundly asleep she took a shower and returning to bed found a slow return to easeful sanity by reading at random in *Pride and Prejudice*. She fell asleep just as the dawn began to pale the stars in the eastern sky and the tiercel out on Hurlstone Point eased the night from him in a wide stretching and beating of his wings. Beside him his mate watched him through one eye and shuffled her feet a little as though in irritation at his waking so soon. When he dropped from the ledge and began a leisurely winging towards the long shingle stretch of the bay she closed her eye and drew her head down into the feathered cover of her tawny mantle.

★　★　★

Alfie Grey and Sir John Warboys met on a seat outside the Festival Hall overlooking the Thames, the brown flood of the tide running in fast. Over the many past years they had had many meetings here and all with the same purpose. They sat together but a little more apart than would two men who had met by appointment. The difference in class between them was quite clear, but had no significance . . . dark suit, bowler hat and neatly rolled, malacca-handled umbrella hob-nobbing in fleeting acquaintance with highly polished, ex-army black boots, heather-brown trousers, a dark blue double-breasted blazer with a British Legion badge, brightly burnished regimental buttons and grey trilby hat sprigged with a tiny slip of blue-green mallard feather.

Warboys said, 'Nice to be with you again, Alfie. Business with pleasure — as usual of course, but the one is always a condiment for the other . . . mustard to flavour the banger, red pepper and a squeeze of lemon to go with the smoked salmon. That river out there used to be full of them in good Queen Bess's royal days. They're coming back too . . . and appropriately in good Queen Bess's royal days.'

'God save the Queen and to hell with all them what don't agree.'

Warboys smiled. 'Royally said. How well do you know North Somerset and the Devon border area?'

'Did a stint at Taunton once. And some night exercises on Exmoor. Wet and windy. But then, there was some nice specimens of

Koelaria cristata . . . no *albescens*. Crested Hair grass. You point me in the right direction, Sir John, and give me a few days to look around and I'm yours faithfully and grateful with it because I fancy a breath of country air. But as you know, Sir John, being a loyal subject of Her Majesty, I like to savvy exactly where I stand. Would he be one of her enemies to confound?'

'Just that.'

'High or low class?'

'High. And one of those with whom it is better to deal privately than publicly. Justice will be done but in camera.'

'Do I do it open? Or, in a manner of speaking, put on the old false moustache?'

'Just be yourself, but keep out of sight as much as you can.'

'Rush job?'

'No. The gentleman concerned has a country estate but also a London house and business. We'd like him to depart this world in the country. Time and place we leave to you — but, if you can, avoid too direct an approach, seize the moment which will arouse the most bizarre or misleading speculations.'

Alfie nodded and then said with honest concern, 'I know it ain't my concern, Sir John. But a man likes to know not why, of course, you want it done, but is it being done to a sort whose, say, wife and family ain't wise to things and would genuinely pipe an eye and place a wreath?'

Warboys shook his head gently from a momentary excess of affection for Alfie, and said, 'You are a nice man, Alfie. And I know how you feel. No, Alfie — he is not a nice man. His wife won't grieve much for him. He has no sons or daughters, but a nephew who will inherit and who will with the resilience of the young mourn him briefly genuinely and a little longer conventionally and then step into his inheritance with the gusto of any reasonable youth who on his birthday morning impatiently wonders which of the many gift-wrapped parcels he should open first.'

Alfie smiled and said, 'You got a nice way of putting things, sir. But what I've always said about you — if you will pardon the liberty, sir — is that you ain't one thing to one kind and another thing to another kind. Whatever you feel you keeps to yourself. And if you'll pardon the liberty, sir — right from the start I set myself up to be like you. The job's the job. You do it. But Alfie, I said to myself — just you always stay Alfie, like Sir John always stays Sir John.'

Warboys chuckled. 'That's one of the nicest

things I've had said to me for years. Thank you, my dear Alfie. And now I must go. You know where to pick up anything you want and your advance on expenses?'

'Of course, sir.'

'And your wife?'

'A nod's as good as a wink. She thinks I go snooping around for hire purchase companies checkin' up on clients. At least I think she thinks that. But with a woman you never can tell. My guess is that they act daft like that for their own comfort and out of loyalty to a man what's trying to turn a far from moral penny. But there it is. My kind is needed.'

'Always has been, Alfie. Open any page of the Old Testament and you realize that.' He stood up and handed Alfie a thickly packed quarto envelope. 'Advance of your fee. And two sheets of information which you sit here and read when I'm gone. That done, tear it in little bits and drop it over Waterloo Bridge as you go home.'

And these instructions, as soon as Sir John Warboys was out of sight, Alfie carried out to the letter. He was a loyal and obedient servant. He read his instructions and the information notes — once read never forgotten — and then, tearing them into small pieces, went up on to Waterloo Bridge and — since the gentle wind was south-westerly — went to the downstream side of the bridge and mid-way over leaned on the balustrade, let a tourist steamer go downstream for Greenwich, a police patrol launch swing down through one arch and make a sharp turn and go upstream through another, and then one by one dropped at intervals like reluctant confetti his ragged scraps of instructions into the King's Reach.

At that moment, as he turned away and made for the top of the Strand, Alfie had no idea what Sir Anthony Swale looked like or what he did in particular but he was quick to remedy this. Once over the bridge he turned right in the Strand and walked down to Fleet Street where he had an old and valued friend — with whom he had shared perilous Monte Cassino days — who was now running the library of a national newspaper. Here he sat happily for well over an hour, reading the clippings about Sir Anthony. Sometimes he shook his head approvingly, and often he pushed up his lower lip towards his nose and frowned, and for a long time he studied the various photographs of the man. Afterwards he took his librarian friend out to a pub lunch where they fought part of the Sicilian Landings over again and then finished by differing good-naturedly over the respective merits in bed of twin sisters they had known who lived in a top floor apartment in a street just behind the Church of Or San Michele — the shrine of all the Arts and Crafts of Florence except the one the girls practised.

Draining half a glass of Guinness in one easy, unhurried swallow, then sighing and putting the glass down, Alfie's friend said sadly, 'Ah, those were the days. Nothing happens now because everything is happening. When it's all one thing then it's nothing, and I mean nothing. Don't you find life gets you down?'

'Aye.' Alfie always made a point of agreeing with his friend.

'Bloody dull. News, news, news — but it ain't news. We've had it all before. Bloody dull. And we all get bloody dull. Everything happens and it's all the same. Big passenger jet crashes. Big news today. Forgotten tomorrow. Dull, dull. I tell you, Alfie — nothing touches the heart or the imagination. Look at you — retired. And now what? Breakfast, dinner, tea, allotment, pub, and once a week a go with the Missus if she'll let you and if you can. Give me Cassino — when you got a break back in Naples every day was a birthday with bells hung all round. Not like now. We got everything and we got nothing.' He grinned. 'Am I depressing you?'

Alfie grinned back. 'Only a bit round the edges. I'll get the missus to iron 'em out. Well — ' he slid off his stool and gave his friend a gentle punch on the chest, 'I'm away. Got a lot of dull things to do.'

'Keep it like that Alfie. Don't want you ending up as one of my press-cuttings.' He winked.

And Alfie winked back.

When Alfie reached home his wife was out. He went up to the attic — which he had converted into his own private snug and workplace — and, though they had no need of it, began to clean his 'equipment' as he called it. He had a lot of equipment and always enjoyed the pleasure of deciding what he should take with him for any particular expedition. Today he was in no hurry, though he half knew at the back of his mind what his choice would be. He suddenly grinned to himself at the memory of a little incident which had occurred not long after he had first begun to work for Sir John Warboys. Some young police constable, new, and wet behind the ears, had picked up a rumour about Alfie's armoury and bent on promotion had called and asked Alfie if he had guns and if so he'd like to see the licences.

'Your super know about this visit?' Alfie had asked.

'No — but what's that to you? Just answer — have you got guns here because if so I'd like to see the licences.'

Alfie said, 'If you want to see anything in here — you'd better go back and get a search warrant.'

'Cheeky, eh? Well, I'll just do that.'

The constable gone, Alfie had telephoned his emergency number and luckily found Sir John Warboys there. The police constable never returned and was, Alfie learned later, transferred the next day to some, no doubt, under-staffed station in another part of the Metropolis.

Now, hearing a noise downstairs, Alfie opened his door and called, 'That you, love?'

'Yes.'

'Got some bad news. Uncle Bill's ill. I got to go off for a while to look after him.'

Knowing more than she would ever admit she called back, 'Are you sure it isn't Uncle Dick that's sick?' She finished with a slightly tipsy laugh that made Alfie smile.

★ ★ ★

The two men sat on individual park chairs facing south across the well trodden grass to the Carriage Road and the Guards' Barracks. Some way behind them the Serpentine

70

water-fowl were busy with mating display and the chasing and harrying of hen birds by cocks and the occasional stand-up miracle of two cocks walking on the water surface, wings spread in brief and mock threat. The returned swallows hawked low over grass and water and the young green leaf of trees and shrubs, as yet untouched by London's grime and Nature's time, shone like polished enamel. One of the men was fair-haired and blue-eyed, big, fresh looking and with a certain handsomeness and wholesomeness of appearance and carriage. When he smiled it came genuinely as from the true spring of some inner innocent pleasure. It also had the same character when it came from the savouring of some contemplated deviousness or brutal stratagem. This was Leo Chukolev and with him was Mikhail Yepikov, short, squat, big-shouldered and long-armed, dark-haired and wearing an habitual frown as though some sun unseen by others was worrying him by its glare. Both of them were close nearing the end of their thirties, and both of them were temporarily attached to the Embassy of the Union of Soviet Socialist Republics at 13 Kensington Palace Gardens, W.8, which was no more than a drive and a seven iron to the west of where they were sitting. Chukolev, who had just sat down to join Yepikov after coming from the direction of the Round Pond, said, 'He's all ready to do it. But there are certain conditions.'

'Money? He wants more?'

'No, Mikhail.'

'Then what?'

'We must supply the device — to his specification. He insists that to fit it the way we want it calls for a design which makes it impossible to detect even, say, if a garage were carrying out a Ministry of Transport check on the car. He has given me drawings.'

'Where do we get it made in this country?'

'We don't. We send the drawings to Moscow. The device is not large and as you know there are other ways of shipping it in to this country than by the diplomatic bag. His Excellency is genuinely to know nothing of this. That is protocol.'

'And where will he fit it? In the garage?'

'Of course not. Our friend, the good Mr Kirkman, always services the car and delivers it back to the mews garage below the flat which Sir Anthony Swale uses when in London. There is a garage key on the ring with the car keys. Already he has made a duplicate. Whenever we tell him he will go into the garage when Sir Anthony is not at home and fit the device. The next time Sir Anthony uses the car and feels like smoking a cigarette . . . Ha, you can imagine! With, it could be, one thumb still pressing on the lighter he goes skywards . . . Eh, eh! If not necessarily heavenwards!'

He leaned back and chuckled exorbitantly.

Mikhail nodded gravely and then suddenly broke into a chuckle and said, 'I think it is very funny and very good. His Excellency . . . well, that is not our business what he thinks. It will be said, of course, that the British have done it because he worked for us.'

'Naturally. If they say anything at all.'

'But why do it at all? Sir Anthony — I have met him sometimes . . . once in Moscow — has always been true to us and we have rewarded him well with money and with many fine pieces of antique jewellery . . . paintings . . . icons . . . So many things, and all so cleverly done that suspicion has never fallen on him. So, I say, why does Moscow tell us to do it?'

'When the horse that has pulled the cart grows old and loses its strength — you sell it for knacker's meat and buy another. There was a time when Sir Anthony was very useful . . . for years and years. Now . . . well, it is only very occasionally he is of use or worth. Also, perhaps, when a man begins to grow old and his sins have increased with age

73

. . . would it not be natural for him to think of making a deal with God or his Government in return for absolution? There is a great deal Sir Anthony could pass on which the British Government would like to know . . . for instance, the names of others far younger than he who begin to ripen towards the fruiting point.' He laughed, suddenly pleased, and said to the other, 'I make a joke in their language, you see . . . *ripen towards the fruiting point*?'

'Yes, very clever. You will perhaps explain more fully later. For now . . . when all this is done — what do we do with your good Mr Kirkman? May not the day come when he, too, could — what you say — about turning to the ripening point?'

'We are not so stupid as that. He works for us. We pay him. He is single man and he goes to Holland to some girl in Amsterdam. For the moment I cannot recall her name. But this I do know — he never ever walk alive off the cross Channel boat to feel her loving arms around him.'

'That is not a likeable thing.'

'True. But the world is full of not likeable things. Be wise. Anyway — that is the word from Moscow.'

⋆ ⋆ ⋆

Maurice Kirkman, forty, going a little bald from the front of his straw-pale hair, complexion rubicund, eyes green, was just under six feet tall, well built and in far better physical condition than most men of his age since he treated his body like a good and valuable friend. He even sometimes alone talked to it as though it were another person in the room with him, calling it Kirky — for he always thought of himself as Maurice and at all the jobs he had ever held had always answered to Morry, Morris and — rarely — More Rice, which was not approved of by him and, if insisted upon, would turn him nasty. And Maurice nasty reverted at once to the two-striper Paratrooper he had more than briefly been only in the end to be invalided out because of a strained heart and consequent shortness of breath. When that happened he grieved for the first time in his life.

His father, who had been a drunkard and had treated him like a dog, fell inebriated off a scaffolding where he was working as a plasterer. His mother — when he was sixteen — just walked out one morning and had never come back and, since his father treated this as something he had long expected, Maurice made no fuss about it either. But as soon as he could he joined the Army. After the Army he worked in a garage and became a skilled mechanic. He was intelligent, as fit as he could possibly be, sober except for very rare, and deliberate, indulgences. He liked women and was attractive to them for his looks, his good manners, and generous virility. Though he would never have said so, he preferred women to men, preferred their company and, deep in his heart, knew that they were fundamentally worthier and more civilized than men. He only had one serious flaw. He had no very great concern with right or wrong. He kept his nose clean in public of course. But given the chance he was always ready to earn a little extra money over his garage pay. He had over the years fallen into spare-time activities which provided the zest which his working-life lacked. He made friends who had friends who sometimes put a little private work his way which broke the monotony of his regular repair and servicing garage routines and helped to increase the bank deposit balance whose growth he watched with the fondness of a father presiding over the increasingly more confident steps of a toddling son. And son, too, he meant to have — but not in this country. In Amsterdam — working as an assistant in a dress shop — there waited for him Katje . . . plump, blonde, and met two years since, when she had come to London briefly as an *au pair* girl. They were meant for one another. Cupid had smiled on them. Thirty miles south of Amsterdam, near Gouda, he knew from her, her parents worked a profitable and extensive polder bounded on one side by a main road with a long disused garage and petrol pump installation.

With the money to come from this Sir Anthony Swale job — and the payment was to be generous — the garage could be re-equipped and he could run it and, when things that way were slack, he could always lend a hand on the holding and heaven would be all around him. Katje's cooking and wifely comfortings would be all he asked, except for the blessing of a child or children who would never have to go through the misery he himself had known.

As for Sir Anthony Swale and the Rolls-Royce, a lovely bit of work — well, a man had to look after Number One. For Sir Anthony — although he tipped well — he didn't care a brass farthing. But for the car . . . ah, well, over that he would grieve a while.

Still, all that was on the side and yet to come . . . and so were a few other things. So far it had all been friendly and no talk or explanation outside the job in hand, and everyone trusting everyone ... all good chums and jolly good company — he didn't think. Once he had done the job and had his money he would be gone.

Holland and Katje, love and kisses, and his Dutch — already adequate — improving every day. Then a small car, and a boat for Sunday canal sailing picnics. His dream — and no bloody child of his ever having to put up with the kind of treatment he had known. Pity, though, he couldn't have got it all honestly. But there you were — a man shouldn't ask too much from life. Just make the best of what came along.

3

Walking through the beeches on the ridge high above his own domain, no shotgun under arm this morning in case he met with vermin for there was a headache with him and a lack of easiness in his body which filled him with a slow anger so that he was in no mood for shooting, Sir Anthony Swale came finally to the end of the track between the smooth, elephantine grey trunks of the beeches and to the stile that took the path through to the high top meadow of Samuel Black's farm. The Spring grass was coming on stronger every day and young Steven Black was working a tractor and fertilizer-spreader over the ground, the light morning air fogging the spread gently behind him like a soft early morning mist.

He pulled up as he came abreast of Sir Anthony and switched off the tractor motor.

'Morning, sir.'

'Morning, Steven.'

He liked the strongly built youth. His chestnut hair had a sheen to it which owed nothing to any lotion or hair cream. He wished he could have had a son like him.

79

'Dad says if I saw you to say that he looked it up in the deeds about that bit of stone-walling at the top of High Copse and it's rightly so that it's his responsibility to keep it in fair nick.'

'Well, that's nice of him. He must have been feeling in a good mood.'

Steven grinned. 'Aye — the lambing's gone well. Nice seeing you, Sir Anthony.'

'And you, Stevie.' And it was. A young chap, moving fast towards manhood. Strong, no bloody nonsense . . . aye and with the girls to come and not hard to draw. Touched with a sudden, warm sentiment and part nostalgia from the memory of his own days at this youth's age, he said, 'You haven't got your own car yet, have you?'

Steven laughed. 'Not yet. Not until I can put it all down in cash. Dad won't let me look at hire purchase. Don't have it until you can pay for it. That's him.'

'Well — there's much to be said for it. Anyway . . . ' He paused . . . God, eighteen and not a worry on his mind, not even as to whether he'd put a girl in the family way after a Saturday dance since most of the maids learned of contraception now about the same time as they learned their catechism. Oh, brave new world which had such forbidden delights in it — and no fear of embarrassment or censure.

He went on, 'Wouldn't like to do something for me, would you?'

'Of course, Sir Anthony, if I can.'

'You can. Lady Swale's got her own car. But there's the Rover and the Mini eating their heads off down there. Not good for horse or car. I'd be glad if you gave them a run for me now and then and — if I ever leave it down here — you can do the same for the Rolls.'

Steven's eyes widened. 'Well, Sir Anthony . . . Gosh, that's . . . Well, I can't believe it. Oh . . .'

'What's the matter?'

'Well, I was thinking about insurance and all that. I might . . . well, not from any fault of mine . . . get into an accident and — '

'Forget it. Everything is insured for anything that can happen. Only one stipulation. No driving if you're over the limit.'

'No, Sir Anthony. I won't do that anyway because I'm near teetotal. I worked it out . . . I mean the money I'd save. Mind you, Sir Anthony, I like a good booze-up when it's called for — but after that, then it's a hired car and driver. Four or five of you share and it comes out cheap. But, sir — '

'Yes?'

'Would you be good enough to give my father a call and tell him? I don't say he'd disbelieve me, but he would appreciate it.'

'Of course I will.'

Walking back to the Hall Sir Anthony, in a sudden and rare mood of self pity, thought . . . where did it all go wrong? Happy family life, wealthy father, public school, University, then ten years in business and a fair fortune made to put alongside the larger one which would come with his father's death — which it did, unexpectedly early, the old boy taking a fall at hunting and breaking his neck on the ground which was as soft as butter almost from long rain and cattle churning. Everything was his and suddenly the flowering came as he found a new world for himself, a world full of beautiful things which his money could buy and yet with much beyond his reach because of regional and political reasons.

Oh, how gently and subtly they had handled that when he had become first a Member of Parliament and then a Junior Minister. Quid pro quos was the name of the game . . . all those years ago. And how well he could remember the first thing — and that sensibly not Eastern European to begin with. An exquisite thing. His first thrill of possession often came back to him, not as

82

intense, of course, but a steady joy, when he held it in his hand — a little nineteenth-century gold *aide memoire* mounted on the outer covers with a pair of miniatures of two girls by Jean Honoré Fragonard. In no way had they ever risked compromising him . . . He was for the most part a post office . . . taking and receiving messages and, fairly often, goods, seldom bulky and always wrapped so that he had little idea of their nature.

It was to be fifteen years before he had met his opposite number at Portofino and that — shades of Horace Walpole — had been a serendipity for she was a woman, Slav and blonde, two years his junior, and deadly and determinedly professional, he was to learn. But with him, during this one and only meeting, an experience which few other women were ever to match. Then, without explanation, someone else took her place . . . someone he had never seen, a name and no more. Those he did see came and went. But, for them all, he had to say there had never been one single moment in his double life when they had embarrassed him or put him ever in the shadow of fear or threat. They'd made a bargain, and the bargain held, had held until now when, to his own pleasure (for it was not something he wished to suggest himself), they had asked him if he would like to retire and enjoy — without any covert commitments — the rest of his life in the pleasant routines of a country gentleman? Did he regret any of it? No. A quirk of time and company had put him on their side. It could easily have not gone that way. And anyway, there was irony behind it all — for nearly everything he had collected was already willed by him to the nation. So virtue was growing to a flowering from the base compost of treachery.

He went down through the trees to the lower meadows, walked along the brookside, then sat on the parapet of the drive bridge and lit a cigarette. As his eyes roamed across the sweep of the park and the yew-lined drive and the glimpse of thc far white house and the rising wooded ground beyond, he smiled to himself with the pleasure he took in owning it all. Through a dark ritual of treason and deceit there had come into his possession so many things of great beauty . . . so many of the works of the great masters . . . Botticelli . . . Pier Angelo . . . Picasso . . . and the Painter of Acropolis . . . of Providence . . . for these no price was too high to pay, no treachery too great and no self-disgust too biting not to be borne. Yet the few simple things he really coveted — a wife's passionate and self-immolating love and a son to follow him — had been denied him. He saw now that long before he had decided to turn traitor the gods had begun to make him pay for his coming treachery. Still . . . even without these there was much left . . . oh, much, much left. Always something new.

And as though to prove him right his eyes were caught by the soaring movement of a bird far to the west and high over Dunkery Hill. For a moment or two it was unremarked . . . a soaring bird . . . and then he recognized it as it drifted on the wind towards him. It was a peregrine, but whether it was a tiercel or a female it was too far away to know. His father's old gardener had owned and trained one but some trigger-happy fool had shot it. Now, *there* would be something to do when his days moved into the sere and yellow . . . find some cliff eyrie — and they were to be found — and take one of the young and train it. He laughed suddenly. Not for him.

He went back and found his wife taking a late breakfast. He kissed her good morning and said, 'I'm going back to London tomorrow. Would you like to come? A week on the town would do you good . . . or at least amuse you.'

She looked up at him and for a moment or two he felt that there was some urge in her to say yes. Then she shook her head and said, 'I'm sorry — but I've got things arranged which I just can't put off.'

Though it was said gently and genuinely as he knew, he felt the pain of rejection sharp in him, but he kept his face and manner unchanged and said with an easiness which surprised him, 'Very well. As you wish.'

★　★　★

Ruth Winslade knew they were there, and had known it for two weeks. Once if not twice a week her Rolls-Royce stood in the Allerford riverside car-park and she walked up to the National Trust bench below Hurlstone Point. She had been sitting there on a morning of high wind, the long stretch of Porlock beach lined with the creaming white bursts of high tide breakers, some of them running up the shingle bank to break over its crest, when the tiercel had come down the long length of the combe and had passed so close to her that she could see plainly the limp form of the partridge he carried. She had been sitting without moving for at least five minutes and he had taken no heed of her. He disappeared as he dropped close over the first of bramble and gorse growth and then the grey rocks and loose shale only to come in sight again out

86

towards the headland point as he swung up from his swift stoop and called. He hovered like a kestrel and called twice more. She saw the falcon come beating out from the cliff face and, with her coming, the tiercel dropped the kill which his mate let pass her and then winged over and stooped to take the limp-winged erratically falling partridge. The tiercel called and slid down the easterly wind to her and then both of them turned and flew round the point and from her sight. Probably, she thought, to some rock or ledge where they took their kills. And pray God that it might be well out of sight.

Walking back down the path to the tree-bordered river she found herself thinking about her recent dinner with Sir Anthony and his . . . she could not repress the judgment though it came edged with charity and love . . . far too acquiescent and meek a wife. He was a man much in the style of her husband. Brightness caught his eye, a new and pretty face raised his ache for possession, a rare or declining breed of beast or bird was high subject for shooting and stuffing or some degrading captivity. Thank God, so far as she knew he never came out this way. Not that they were so rare but because they were so beautifully what they were . . . another part of God's handiwork. The lust in some men reached far beyond the simplicity of a neighbour's wife or present day Helen . . . or Cleopatra. The greed of Midas had widened . . . fur, feather and hide.

As she crossed the footbridge to the car Tom Honnicot folded the morning paper he had been reading as he sat in the driving seat of the Rolls and got out to open the rear door for his mistress.

When she came up to him and was about to get into the car, Honnicot's one hand holding the door the other reaching for her elbow, she stopped her movements and looking over her shoulder, said, 'My goodness, Tom — it's a long time since I've seen one like that.'

He smiled. 'You're right, ma'am. Been looked after for a few years that has. Like this one — ' he nodded to the high polish of the Rolls-Royce's bonnet. 'Old Rover it is. Nice sort of bloke has it too. It's the apple of his eye.'

'Do you know him?'

'Never seen him in my life before. Drove in just after you went for your walk. Pleasant, mild sort of man. Friendly and full of talk, too.' He laughed. 'He's gone up the other path towards Selworthy — and I don't think you could guess what for.'

'Then tell me.'

88

'He collects grasses.'

'Grasses?'

'Yes, ma'am. I felt surprised like you did. We got chatting and he said he was a Londoner on holiday — and collecting. So I said collecting what? He sort of grinned and said 'Among other things, grasses'. Then he walks over to the bank there and comes back with a stalk of grass in his hand and puts it in front of my nose and says, 'Wot's that then?' And when I said a bit of grass he said 'No, it isn't.' He said it was Festucco something or other. Then he told me its ordinary English name — Squirrel-tail Fescue. He's a grass collector, ma'am.'

Mrs Winslade laughed and said, 'Well, that sounds harmless enough. Though I suppose given enough collectors then grass could become a protected plant. And Honnicot — ' She eyed him seriously for a moment or two and then went on, ' — you and I understand one another and I know you've got eyes in your head and so far have said nothing not even to me.'

'That's right, ma'am. But there's few around here would pay much attention. They'd think they came from Countisbury. Not nesting here. Don't worry, ma'am.'

'Thank you Honnicot.' She half turned and looked at the Rover and smiled. 'I do like to see things well kept. I'm sure he's a very nice man indeed.'

★   ★   ★

It was Sunday morning. Distantly from down the valley came the regularly spaced tolling of the five-minute bell from the church. Margery Grant came down the footpath from the farm carrying the picnic basket in one hand and her raincoat slung over her shoulder.

Steve Black smiled to himself from the sheer pleasure of looking at her. So many things, he thought, were so good to look at . . . like the way the swallows under his father's barn eaves dropped in fast half loops and came to rest from speed to settle feather-light on the edge of their mud-scallops of nests . . . like the way a mare would suddenly throw up her head and whinny and race across the meadow slope to come to him at the field gate, mane flying and foal long-legging at her side, and then the velvet feel of his hand against her warm nose as she nudged him for the apple she knew he had somewhere for her . . .

And now his girl. She came down the farm lane, long dark hair taking the gentle surge and fall of her shoulders, sun gleams sliding

90

over it and — even though she walked in gum boots against the lane's muddiness from night rain, her good shoes in the basket — she seemed less to touch the stone rough ground that to skim it, walking, it seemed, an inch above the common earth, floating like an angel. Not that he would put it like that to anyone else. Fancy talk didn't go down with his family . . . vets' fees and crop yields and prices and in season the calendar of hunt meets and Somerset's chances in the John Player Cricket League. One day he was going to marry this girl . . . one day he was going to be full farmer himself and one day he was going to have sons and daughters and . . . Oh, well . . . One day, one day. Who cared about that now? There was only this day.

She stopped and looked at him and then the car.

'Where'd you get that?'

'Bought it. Won the pools.'

'Liar. 'Tis Sir Anthony's Renault. I'd know it anywhere.'

'That's right. He said would I give his cars a run round while he was away. Lady Swale only uses her own. He's got half a dozen up there. I thought I'd start at the bottom and work up.'

'You're not kidding me along?'

'Get in and stop worrying and when you're

settled give me a kiss or you can just get out again and go home.'

'It's like that?'

He grinned. 'Take it or leave it.'

She got in, gave him a brief kiss, escaped the further movement of his hands and arms and said, 'Where are we going?'

'To Paradise, me dear — and never coming back.'

They laughed together and then she suddenly leaned across and kissed him on the side of the mouth and felt for a moment or two his mouth turning to take hers fully and his hands, strong yet gentle, running over her breasts.

Some way up the valley to Exford they met Lady Swale hacking back from her morning ride. Steve Black pulled in to the side to let her pass. She reined in for a moment or two.

'Off for a Sunday picnic?'

'Yes, ma'am. We thought we'd go up over the Tops and see if we can pick up some plovers' eggs. Pity Sir Anthony isn't down — he could have had what we get. He's been very kind in letting me have the car.'

'He'd have liked that. But I think it will be some while before he's back. He's gone to Paris. To see some specialist. He's not been well lately.'

'Is it anything serious, ma'am?'

'I don't know. He gets very bad asthma at times — and he's always trying new cures. I think that's what this visit is all about. He's found something new he can try.'

As she rode on, hearing the sound of their car dying in the distance behind her, she gave a little sigh as the memory came to her of her early days with the man she was to marry. All had been rose-coloured and each day the beginning of new joys and the rising higher of her tide of happiness. All that . . . so long ago, it seemed. And now here she was older and wiser and, so it seemed, not one but two people. The one of this morning when she had risen to the golden promise of a mid Spring day . . . the morning full of bird song, the faint breeze through her half-open window already touched with warmth and full of the scents from the blooming of the Ena Harkness roses across the front of the house below her window. How would it have been to have awakened with a man, a beloved one, still caught in the net of night's drowsiness at her side . . . to have been awake before him, to have leaned over and watched the sleeping face while tenderness and love rose slowly through her like a warm tide of joy . . . Aye, perhaps to have fallen into the sly trap of love, to find him — no sleeper — only feigning such — slowly opening his eyes and smiling and reaching for her, for her body, for her caresses, for her love.

The mood was broken as a young rabbit broke cover across the road before her and her mount snorted, made a short side passage, and then settled to steady gait.

As she went up the drive to the house she saw Richard Crane in the front garden of the cottage pushing a lawn mower to cut the grass of the small patch which had once been a vegetable garden.

She reined in and as he came to the fence and gave her a good morning she said, 'There's no need for you to do that. Preston would come down and do it.'

'He did offer. But I like doing it.' He grinned. 'After being a troglodyte most of the week I like to be doing something in the open. Have you had a good ride?'

'Yes, thank you.'

'And Sir Anthony — how is he?'

'I haven't heard anything more.' Then with a sudden, unexpected upsurge of feeling, she said, 'But I can't think it's anything serious. There are doctors and specialists in London as good as any in Paris.'

Crane laughed. 'Surely he wouldn't want any excuse to go to Paris and — '

He broke off suddenly as he saw the look which had come over her face. For a moment they faced one another in silence, the mare fidgeted a little, and then she said frankly, 'He always needs an excuse. That's the oddness of his temperament. Nothing is straightforward — not even the nature or shape of his sins. You know only one Sir Anthony Swale — and that the best of them all. The lover and collector of beautiful things . . . a true lover. But there's no woman in the world who could rouse and keep his love the way . . . well, the way a painting or a fine piece of antique jewellery or sculpture does.' Carried away unexpectedly and unable to resist the powerful need to face someone else with the truth . . . even to shout it aloud, she went on, 'Don't think that great cellar is full of stuff which he has forgotten or even half-forgotten about. He knows everything down there and he loves everything down there with a love that is satisfied just with the fact of possessing. That is the only kind of love he knows and the only kind he wants.' She stopped short there and suddenly smiled at him. Then she went on in her normal voice, still partly smiling, 'He would have me in his collection. Wanted me there so badly that he married me. And I was too young to read his nature until it was too late. But there are some things which are outside time and convention for which it is never too late. Like tenderness and understanding.'

The silence held between them for a moment or two and then Crane smiled, raised his arms and clasped his hands across the back of his head and said in a normal voice, 'You are telling me something I know already. I may have spent a great deal of my life in cellars and museums and sale rooms — but all you have spoken about is there already. Pictures always come before words. Pictures man had before he had words. And here and now — we need no words of the kind you mean.'

She laughed suddenly and began to urge her horse into movement. Then, turning, she looked back at him and said, almost gaily, 'All right — then let us forget about words. Become children again and content ourselves with sharing a picture book.'

He watched her go and then, with a heavy shrug of his shoulders as he turned to the lawn mower, he said to himself, 'You're mad. Anyway, she'll probably think better of it.'

* * *

Sunday afternoon, the sky blue, the sunlight, like a benison, falling impartially on one and all of the people enjoying the green grass and the faint leaf stir of the trees as a mild breeze came across the Serpentine in Hyde Park. Colour and movement, laughter, children shouting and running, and an airliner from Heathrow marking a great white chalk score across the blue, and here and there couples lying together in erotic embraces . . . all so simple and all so ordinary . . . so nice, all these people individually, mostly, but so stubborn as a race sometimes . . . never knowing when to give up . . . never knowing the right moment to say *enough*, thought the dark-haired, habitually frowning Mikhail Yepikov. And so devious — particularly those of high rank and birth, men of great possessions and wealth. Like Sir Anthony Swale — though some credit had to be his for he had served them well, even if, unlike most, he had called for payment, and high payment, and much of that in Mother Russia's treasures . . . Ah, but they would all come back one day . . .

A voice behind him said, 'Hi, Micky! Nice little breeze goin'. Can't keep your eyes off the girls on the grass, eh? Don't tell me they don't allow that kind of thing in Moscow, eh? Tug the old skirt around till the zip's in the front. Awful places parks. No decency.'

As Maurice Kirkman sat down beside the Russian he gave him a playful, soft punch on

97

the shoulder, knowing he would like to make it the real thing, and said, 'Sorry I'm a bit late. Had to wait for a bus — forgot it was the Sunday service. You got the doings then?'

Mikhail said, 'You are very jokey, yes?'

'Oh, yes. Very jokey.'

'Last time you come from that direction.' He nodded towards the Horse Guard Barracks.

'So I did. But variety's the spice of life. Walk the same path on every patrol and you'll buy one in the end.'

'Not understand that.'

'Never mind. You got the doings?'

'The mechanism, yes.' He tapped a brown paper parcel which rested on the seat at his side.

'Bit small, isn't it? There enough wallop in that to do the job?'

'Wallop . . . ?'

'Kick . . . Bang . . . Whammo . . . Enough to lift him out of his seat and send him skywards in tiny pieces?' Which, thought Kirkman as he finished talking, would be something I'd like to see happen to a lot of people.

'It is more sufficient. Also there are instructions in English, of course. For the fitting. Very good fitting. Quite small. And there is a diagram for the wirings.'

'When do I fit it?'

'As soon as possible. Sir Swale is now in Paris for some days. We know because though he is there for other reasons he is also there for us to do something . . . I mean to do something for us.'

'He's got a chauffeur. Say he comes along, takes the car out and lights a coffin nail?'

'Coffin nail — what is that?'

'Cigarette.'

'Oh . . . No. He is a non-smoker and, anyway, he is on holiday while Sir Swale is in Paris. Only Sir Swale smokes in the car.'

'It's going to make a tricky wiring job. I got to take this away and study it. Won't take long.'

'You do it this evening?'

'Don't be daft. Tomorrow evening, maybe. Or the next for certain. You got Sir Anthony in your pocket. He's in Paris for you. You see he stays there until I give you the all clear.'

'How you do that?'

'Well, not by bleedin' telegram or the phone. Sunday today. You be here same time for the next three days. All right?'

'Yes.'

'Good. And don't fuss. Whoever lights a cigarette with the car lighter blows the whole boiling to kingdom come. You ever thought that someone else might use it when your precious Sir Anthony Swale wasn't in the car?'

'Naturally.'

'Oh, good for you. And so what?'

Mikhail smiled. 'It is obvious. The British Government want to get rid of him. We tell him that. What can he do? He knows it could be the truth. He knows too that the British Government want no scandals about traitors in high places. They will let him run and we will retire him to be a good, honest country gentleman like he has always been. But . . . these are not things for you to worry your head on. Between governments there are often at the end of the day many curious agreements and showing of blind eyes.'

'Shutting.'

'Ah, so. Shutting. So you are quite happy?'

'Delirious.'

'And with all done you go away from England for ever?'

'You bet. This country's sinking and I can't swim.' He gave Mikhail a friendly punch on the shoulder and stood up, and said, 'And the money? You fixed that the way I wanted?'

'Yes, we do that yesterday — all paid to the Amsterdam account of the young lady as you wished.'

'I don't doubt you — but I'll check that before I even open this little surprise gift.' He played a swift tattoo with his fingers over the parcel. Then, giving Mikhail a big wink, walked away seeing Katje and her golden tresses, in a fourteen-footer heeling to a nice breeze, going down the Noordzee Kanaal.

One day there would be a young Kirkman to look after, make things for, show the ropes and teach to take nothing on trust in this rotten, stinking world except those in the tight circle of one's own family. Survival begins at home — that was his not unreasonable motto. And never take anything for granted. He telephoned Katje at her lodgings that evening and she confirmed the arrival of the money.

★ ★ ★

They sat together in the lee of a stone wall, the moorland running away from them, gorse and heather marked here and there with the slow movement of cropping sheep, staid and placid, while about them played and cavorted the small parties of the year's new lambs. They had eaten their picnic lunch and drunk a fair part of the cheap bottle of white wine he had provided. His hand held hers and, as he watched the distant hovering of a hunting kestrel, he felt the slow, caressing movement of her fingers moving over his. He knew her

101

moods and could read the scantiest of her body signals. They were of an age and had ridden the school bus to their first mixed school and then gone to grammar school together. He had never looked elsewhere, but she in the past had teased him with a pretence of favouring someone else, though never to the point of really wounding him.

He moved so that his lips were close to the warmth of her neck and said, 'Father's going to buy the Martins' place when it comes up. Old Martin's got that son in New Zealand and he's all for selling up and going out there. The house is nice, though he's let the land go back here and there . . . but a couple of years would fix that. Shall us go back round by there? Nice social visit. Old Martin'll be pleased.' He laughed. 'He's got an eye still for a pretty girl. Would you like to?'

'If that's what you want.'

'Why don't you ever say what you want?'

She laughed and bent over and kissed his lips briefly. 'I don't have to. I want all you want — but some of it we've just got to wait for.'

'There's some things we could have without waiting. Not serious things, but nice things. I'm with you about the real thing. I can wait. But what's wrong with touching and . . . well, you know what I mean. I love you. I don't want nothing wrong between us, but I tell you this . . . ' He shifted round a little until he hung half over her, his hands on her shoulders, his face over hers so that, like a tiny miracle of a mirror, he saw himself reflected in her eyes' pupils, a distant figure, ' . . . I'd like to kiss 'ee. Not just on the lips . . . but on under your chin . . . your neck and down . . . and down . . . ' He fell silent, watching her, knowing there was no true reading of her mood.

She grinned and said, her voice thick with emotion and deliberate emphasis of her country accent, 'And what else, me dear? What be'ee after pinin' for?'

He was silent for a while, trying to fathom and measure her mood and not minding his uncertainty, knowing that, even in marriage, it would always be there to heighten the joy of their love feast.

He said bluntly, 'I want to kiss your titties. I want to have them in my hands. I want to kiss 'em and then to hold them while I kiss you. No more than that.'

She sat up and turned squarer to him, dark eyes full of humour, and tenderness moving her forward to touch his near cheek with a moth-brushing caress of her lips as she undid the buttons of her shirt blouse and lay back, holding the material away from her breasts.

Then, as he hesitated, not yet on terms with this unexpected love victory, she cried almost with anguish, 'Oh, Stevie . . . Stevie . . . Come on! Come on!'

He slipped his arms around her waist and, as he bent to kiss her, felt the fingers of one of her hands move over the nape of his neck and strongly press his face towards her breasts.

Three thousand feet above the tiercel saw them and was untouched with any interest in them. He marked the thin line of the infant river below, white curded over its low falls from recent rain. He marked the small birds of the gorse and bracken, the stone and whinchats and — something which only a few of the local moorland people knew enjoyed the hospitality of the burgeoning heather and ling and the rising growth of grasses — a covey of black grouse suddenly take flight and go bracken high across the steep hillside to be lost beyond the old mine workings above Simonsbath.

He kissed her and as his lips wandered passionately over her warm, velvet soft flesh there was a swift impatience in him for the future. But for these moments and this benison he knew only joyful gratitude.

It was only fifteen minutes later as they sat up and he lit himself a cigarette as she buttoned up her blouse and then, small mirror in hand, began to touch up her lips that he realized that this was the first of the many times he had taken her out when she had not worn a brassiere. Suddenly he had a sense of awe and amusement and he could hear his father saying — 'Don't you make no mistake, my lad. When it comes to knowing and getting what they want and that, of course, mostly because of love — though bad luck to any man when it ain't — well, we men be babies in arms. I runs this farm like me father and grandfather and others before them — but all on 'em, me included, is run by our women. Don't ever admit it to 'em — but it be so and it behoves a man to shape himself to the fact.'

Putting out a hand and with his knuckles gently touching the side of her face, he said, 'Shall we go back by Martin's place?'

'Yes, why not. But not just yet.'

Silent for a moment, still taking in the warm run of joy which touched spirit and body, he reached out a hand and took one of hers and raised it, awkwardly, to his lips and kissed it, first on the back and then, turning it over, in the cradle of her palm. And it was a kiss that fired her senses so that a slow shiver of nameless origin moved through her, waking every nerve and muscle to the expectancy of fast following ecstasy. He turned then and gently pressed her back again to the springy turf, his full want clear in his eyes, and under the caress of his hands she knew that she had no defence against him.

★   ★   ★

Alfie Grey was bored, and that was a state of mind which gave him no pleasure. A telephone call to Sir John Warboys from his Minehead hotel had brought him the information that Sir Anthony Swale was in Paris and that it might be a little while before he returned home. For the time being Sir John had said it was better for him to remain in the West Country.

This, he thought, was one of the common drawbacks of this kind of job. Hanging around, waiting . . . sometimes days, sometimes weeks. In a way, he supposed, he ought to give it all up and retire. He had no need of the money, and Sir John Warboys would understand. He could say that about Sir John: he was a man full of understanding — but, Lord love us, a gentleman old Nick himself would take his hat off to when it came to a matter of devilry. And all done, though never openly, in the name of the Government. If it was true that God saw everything, then by this time he must be sick and tired and bored with the whole thing. In a way, he suddenly thought to himself, he was in something of the same league, but umpteen divisions lower. Watching people and how they did, and *who* they did and — the trickiest bit — *why* they did. You didn't have to have the whole thing spelt out in capital letters. See a bloke going down a street lined with parked cars, sauntering as though he were enjoying the leisure of a fine, sunny day — though it might be freezing hard — and his right hand dropping to try each door handle as he went by. Watch him when he found one that moved . . . Mum in a hurry to do her shopping, kids bawling from the back seat, can't wait to get to the shops and sweeties and all the muck they stuff down their throats . . . tough tittie. He's in, some quick and expert fiddling, and he's away. Now and again the key is obligingly in the ignition lock. And later ma returning with the kids baa-lambing after her and not able to believe her eyes at the sight of no car. And, Christ Almighty, what's the old man going to say?

Two days after speaking to Sir John, as though the gods had decided to take an interest in Alfie's comforts, as he came along a small upper road that overlooked the valley he passed a small thatched cottage with a notice in front of it announcing that it was free for furnished holiday lettings. It sat on the edge of a bluff overlooking the valley below and gave as fine a view of the Swale estate as a man could wish ... the whole place laid out as though it were a model in a showcase.

Alfie went immediately to the agents in Minehead, took it for a month — paid in advance — gave Sir John Warboys' name as a reference and within two hours drove back preceded by an agency clerk who opened the place up for him, showed him how everything worked, and advised him to air the bedding from the bathroom cupboard in front of the sitting room's electric fire. When he asked was Alfie down on holiday or business he got the answer — 'A bit of both, laddie, but also generally recuperating.'

So Rose Cottage became temporarily Alfie's. He was well content for he had comfort, privacy and one of the finest views in the valley of Swale Place from its ornamental main gates to the wooded crests of the hills that sheltered it from the cold easterly winds of winter. And, also his, was the great convenience of a pay telephone for his own use and through which his employers could readily reach him — though he had never known them do that unless it was something really urgent. The cottage, he considered, put him in clover, made his work easier, and gave him a bird's eye view of Swale Place . . . every movement his to note and if necessary to act on.

Like today after a pint of lager and a Cornish pasty in Dunster and then up here at Rose Cottage sitting comfortably, polishing the lens of the old Zeiss — been times, of course, when he'd preferred, because of distance, a telescope, though not his own — Sir John always provided that and . . . What was that joke? The one he always overdid a bit? Yes . . . *One day some bright man will invent one of these that reads minds and that will be the end of the world.* Quite right, too, when you came to think of it. However, just seeing was enough for the human bloody race at the moment, and some of the things to be seen . . . well, well.

At half-past three (hc was always particular about times for often Sir John insisted on them) she had come out through the glass doors on to the terrace. Big stone urns with fresh potted-out geraniums. White and red in alternate pots. Couldn't stand 'em himself because of the smell. Still they didn't give him hay-fever like bloody cats did. One within three feet and his eyes streamed as though he'd just lost his nearest and best.

Nice blooms these were, though . . . flower heads as big as cricket balls. Sauntered . . . a good word, but perhaps not quite right. No, she idled across the lawn to the drive, but not down it. Right across it into a shrubbery, and she moved a bit quicker now, knowing where she was going and wanting to be there. The things you could tell about people by the way they walked. She was in and out of his lens like something watched on a film. And then in the clear for a while as she followed the line of the fence of the home paddock and so into the small yard at the back of the old gate-keeper's cottage. No gate-keeper now. Only the picture expert bloke that worked for Sir Anthony Swale. And that had been that. Except that it hadn't. He turned the glasses away. Forget the whole thing . . . Why not? He was a honeyswakeymallipants sort of a man and had gone back to his favourite outdoor game for whiling away watching time. Seeing how many different grasses he could name through the glasses without moving from where he was.

Plenty, but nothing out of the ordinary . . . Lesser and common quaking grass . . . some way off and flowering yet, though . . . common bent and velvet bent . . . ditto for flowering . . . but some meadow foxtail in full flower, not that most people would call it a flower . . . almost, and he wasn't ashamed of the thought, like a fairy's chimney sweeping brush.

A movement caught his eye some time later as he half-turned to ease his sitting position. With the reflex action gained over long years his binoculars were up and no need to fine focus them for it was all as plain as if he had been sitting in a cinema. And all in colour.

The cellar bloke had come to the bedroom and was standing there just in his shirt-tails, his hands raised and holding the edge of each curtain to pull it. And behind him . . . well, most jobs usually produced some turn-up for the book, but he would never have laid money on this one . . . was the lady herself almost through taking her clothes off as made no difference and certainly no doubt of the interpretation of the scene.

The curtains were pulled and stayed that way for some long time . . . so long in fact that after a while he got up and took a stroll for a few minutes along the woodland path to ease his muscles. When he returned the curtains were drawn back.

Half an hour later she left the lodge by the way she had come. A little while after that the man came out, a long-handled hoe in his hand, and began to attack the weeds in the strip of flower border that ran parallel with the drive. A thrush somewhere began to tune up for its evening performance and a high flying jet drew a long white score across the blue.

★　★　★

Far away in London Maurice Kirkman finished going over the four sets of plans which had been included in his package. He could read blueprints with the ease and almost the same pleasure he might take from some erotic paperback. The boys in the far East with snow on their boots had done a good job . . . a very good job. The plans were so good they raised no query in him and the device so neat and slim-lined that it was hard to credit the punch that it packed. Concealing the wiring was no problem, but fixing the explosive package — hardly bigger than a large slab of chocolate — would be difficult. Child's play with a ramp to run the car up on. However . . . he was used to working in tight and cramped positions . . . those were the places you got handed to you when you did your apprenticeship. And anyway there was no forgetting the money — a bank transfer to a special account already opened in Amsterdam by Katje. He would do the wiring tomorrow evening. Sir Anthony's chauffeur, whenever his master was away without the Rolls, came in once a day to check that things were all right in the flat, and usually at the same time . . . half-past five . . . for a look around the garage below and then took a quiet stroll to catch the opening of the pub around the corner and the first of the two bottles of Guinness he drank before making his way home across Lambeth Bridge to Jonathan Street and a loving wife. Neither of them cared for the country and so were well pleased that Sir Anthony very seldom wanted their services down in Somerset.

★   ★   ★

She sat a little to one side of the French windows which opened on to the paved run of the terrace that fronted the formal garden, its beds laid out in a great circle at whose centre lay a water-lily pool with a fountain of three mermaids lifting a small cherub aloft with one arm raised holding a goblet from which gushed a great fan-shaped spray of water to cascade over the figures and set the lily pads and blooms to gentle movement.

There was no excitement in her as she waited for Richard Crane and for this she was glad. She had no need for high emotion, no want even for some edge of guilt to excite her

113

feelings. All she craved was the solace of another's understanding, the giving of comfort and the sense, so vital to her deep need, of knowing, no matter what his reason — sensual, sympathetic, or pitying — that here was a man to whom the gift of her body and the tenderness of her touching were not received with unspoken but bodily evident male arrogance, but with a simple joy which stirred first her spirit and then, without haste, her body. No one — and there had been two or three before her marriage — had ever handled her with so much tenderness and long-drawn caresses. His mouth against hers, hungry but not devouring, his hands moving over her nakedness in the same way as she had in the cellar seen him caress some bronze nymph or the marble head and shoulders of a classical goddess.

They had spoken little. Her need lay not then in words, no matter how kind, and his response, though commandingly male yet gentle, had held her in the long swell of the smooth tide of passion they had raised in one another.

When he came now, across the formal garden, the lowering sun catching the high spraying play of the fountain and conjuring from it fast living and dying infant rainbows, she knew that he would listen to her words and recognize them as though he had heard them all before in some dream. She could take no more. For the sake of her pride she could not move through the dusty ritual of married life. And she knew what he would say, and so sensible the words would be, so honest. What they had had, and might have for a while longer, was the gift of time and place and the wanting all falling together. Some of the world's gifts of common kindness to those in true and overriding need, not simply of the flesh-bond, though that followed as warmth stirred the closed bud to opening, but to those who, at some vital moment of their life, had been seduced by the gifts arrayed for their choosing yet had lacked the experience and knowledge to choose wisely. Thus her mother: 'My dear girl . . . what does it matter if they say things about him? Perhaps there is a little truth in it but mostly it is envy. And anyway — with marriage all that would change. I hesitate to be coarse, but plain speaking never hurt anyone. Why should a man go to the expense and trouble of seeking abroad that which he can command at home? And anyway, if sometimes, just sometimes he does — then ignore it. Count your blessings, and know this — there are very few saints who walk this world, and those who do are rarely concerned with marriage. Marriage is a commodity in the human market place. *Caveat emptor.*'

He came in sharply from the right of the terrace so that she had no warning of his approach. He was smiling and the joy in him seemed to have lightened his step and graced what before had been a certain gaucheness in his movements. He came up to her, smiling, glanced back over his shoulder to see that they were not observed from outside, and then bent and kissed her on the forehead, took her right hand and gently placed a small egg in it.

'A gift . . . a swallow's egg. They're nesting under the cottage eaves. The sparrows must have ragged one of the nests out. I found it in the flower bed. This was the only egg unbroken, so I blew it for you and now I gift it to you with, dare I say it, my love?'

She shook her head and was suddenly unembarrassed and outspoken. 'It is better to say nothing special. It happened. It may happen again. And although I do not love him I know I am sinning. I am happy to tell you that were I free and you wished it I would marry you because I know I could love you. But now as a married woman I have sinned and know that I have in me the will and desire to sin so again. But I shall try not to let this be.' She smiled suddenly, moved to a

116

gentle laugh and went on, 'Do not look so solemn. Go, help yourself to a drink and bring me one. Dry sherry. Oh, and by the way — Sir Anthony telephoned a while ago. He's coming back from Paris the day after tomorrow. He asks that you go up and meet him because there's a Sotheby's viewing he wants you to go to with him. He said something about a Fabergé desk-set.'

'Ah, yes. I've seen the advance notice. It's a silver mounted nephrite desk-set in Empire style. Oh, that'll be quite an outing.'

She laughed and said, 'There you see — there's your true love. And don't be put out because I say so. It is as it should be. Let us both be contented now and then with a little comfort on the side.'

He brought her drink and stood with it outheld for her to take and said, 'Please don't mind that I ask you this. But in the beginning . . . with Sir Anthony was it . . . was it love?'

Without hesitation she said, 'Yes, I thought so and that is what makes it so . . . so wasteful. Just for a while love was there for us both.' She paused and then laughed softly. 'Oh, come — please don't look so tragic. You asked and I told you. You know you must not see me as a pitiable figure. I suffer in a great deal of comfort and luxury, which I enjoy. I think it would be hypocritical to deny it.

Now, let us talk no more of ourselves. Tell me — what is nephrite?'

He laughed. 'It comes from the Greek *nephros*, a kidney. Nephrite is a particular sort of black jade . . . so called because it was once held to be a charm against kidney complaints. Did he say which day he wanted me to go up?'

'No. He said he would ring you from London and then you could both come back together in the Rolls.' She smiled. 'He'll probably get you to drive.'

He came across to her and briefly laid the back of his hand against her warm cheek. She reached up and took it, brought it to her mouth and, for a moment or two, set her teeth on his index finger and bit into the flesh gently, but as she did so her eyes were lowered so that she saw past him the run of the formal gardens and beyond them the rising hill slope and she remembered then that it had been as they walked the grassy ride between the massed rhododendrons that she had once told her husband that she was carrying his child. In the weeks that followed until her miscarriage he had been a changed man . . . gentle, considerate, and always anxious about her well-being and comfort. For a time . . . she could think so now without emotion . . . she had been one of his

118

precious pieces come to life, cold ivory turned to warm flesh, touching genuine emotion in him so that for a while there had also been a true love between them . . . but, alas, of such brief flowering . . . and he, a Pygmalion disappointed, turning away as his gentle love gave place to the sporadic, almost violent outbursts of lustful possession. There, she knew, lay his ineradicable flaw . . . the rise of emotions, gentle and true, soaring too soon and too far — and with growth producing distortions which she could not accept.

★ ★ ★

Alfie Grey was not a man to become easily bored. Waiting was more often than not the hallmark of most jobs . . . particularly this kind. But since this one, as in the past with some others, clearly showed all the signs of dragging on for some while, he had had to work out a sensible routine for himself, and that routine was not one which would raise in people any deep curiosity or even idle wondering. When he had to face a direct question — which only happened rarely since he kept very much to himself — he said truthfully that with a partner in London — in fact his wife's brother — he had started a little business. Provide us with a photograph of a lost one ... father, mother, son or daughter — and for a reasonable fee, varying according to the size and the framing, his partner in London would paint a true likeness in oils and specified colouring. And how often would there not be in some sales visit varying opinions as to the colour of long departed Uncle Malcolm's hair, or a little tiff over eye-colouring ... but few could resist the chance to bring a humble touch of the National Portrait Gallery into their homes.

Yet even with this as a side line — and no concession from Sir John Warboys coming from the plea that it could be weeks, maybe months, if the job had to be done down here. 'It's all right, Sir John,' he had recently pleaded, 'but I am getting bored. The target's away and I know this place inside out. You're paying me well, but I don't want you to waste your money. I could come back and do the job in London.'

'No, down there. And a nice long shot — maybe in a place where he won't too soon be seen so that you can come back and be digging your allotment perhaps even before he is found. And don't think you're taking money on false pretences from us. Waiting time is the hard time. And, anyway, the longer you wait the more business you do. Who is to suspect your true profession? You a man of such gentle pursuits — one of the country's foremost experts on English grasses and a lover and connoisseur of those inoffensive growths, the death of which would mean the death of the world. So stay, and play your part. You are safe enough since, to quote the Bard — *There is no art to read the mind's construction in the face . . .* '

So Alfie stayed, partly bored and partly occupied, and with plenty of spare time on his hands which he used to further his collection of grasses — for which pastime he had found an ideal spot. He would drive to Bossington, park his car and then make the round walk sometimes up the hill to Selworthy first and then down the broad combe to Hurlstone Point and so back to his car along the cliff and river path to his starting point. Other times he did the walk in reverse. He collected grasses and made friends with Mrs Winslade for they often met either in the car park or at the National Trust seat below Hurlstone Point. He would sit down a few feet from her and — since after a few meetings he could sense her mood — would either start talking or just give her a good day and amuse himself by putting his binoculars to his eyes and taking a look at the broad scene laid out before him . . . a long incurving arc mostly of shingle beach running

121

west from Hurlstone to distant Gore Point.

One afternoon, a few days after his plea to Sir John, he came down Hurlstone Combe from Bossington Hill and found Mrs Winslade sitting watching the shingle stretch along which a high wind and an incoming tide were making a great bow of creaming, curded breakers. He sat down well away from her, gave her a little nod, and then let his eyes run over the grey fall of the cliff point and to the stretch of breaking rollers on the beach.

Today Mrs Winslade gave him a smile and a nod to which he returned, 'Good afternoon, ma'am.'

'Good afternoon, Mr Grey. Have you found any new grasses for your collection?'

He smiled. 'Ah, you remembered me telling you that, eh? Well, no I haven't.'

'What made you collect grasses? I should have thought there were far more interesting things.'

'I'm sure there are, ma'am. But most of the other things come expensive — or I don't think they should be collected.' He looked at her quizzically for a while, then smiled and went on, 'Shall I be honest with you? You're a nice lady.'

She smiled. 'Are you only honest with nice ladies?'

He laughed. 'Well, there's a teaser. But

honesty don't go by sex, or poor or rich. But to come to the point — what I really collect is people. An' it's the best of all collectings 'cos you don't have to shoot or pick them or fish for 'em. You just look at 'em and then remember them. Now the first time I ever sat on this seat alongside you — you started to worry about me. I couldn't think why — until the second time we met up here and you got the same worrying look and that time I knew because I'd been up here in between on me own and seen 'em.'

'Seen what?'

'Your birds. Them down there.' He nodded in the direction of the rock fall and cliff drop. 'Then I knew. You thought I might be also an egg collector, or have pals what were. Now be honest, didn't you, ma'am?'

'Well, how was I to know that you were too good and decent a man to be such?'

'Well, thanks for the compliment, which I know is truly meant and gladly taken. Anyway, I looked 'em up in Minehead Library. And I can say you did the right thing. Why, if coming down the combe there I found a patch of *Carex stenolepsis* — which would be real out of place, I can tell you, since, aside from being quite rare, it's found more or less only in Argyll, Perthshire and Angus — do you think I'd tell any Tom, Dick

123

or Harry? Wot — ' he mimicked a voice far commoner than his own ' — here's a funny looking bit of stuff. The missus would like that for her dry grass arrangement in the parlour. And up it comes root and all.'

Mrs Winslade laughed, and then said, 'You make me very happy, Mr Grey.'

'Then that's good. And, let me say, *Carex stenolepsis* isn't funny looking at all. It's a nice looking thing. So there — no more worries.'

'I never really did. But . . . '

'Aye, leave it there. You never knows in this life. You think they got eggs and will have babies?'

'I hope so. They've got a nest site — you can't see it from here or from the beach. You'd have to watch the birds to see where they go. So, anyone who watched long enough could find it.' She paused for a moment and then with a warm smile went on, 'I wonder, Mr Grey . . . would you like to come and have tea with me one afternoon? Just the two of us . . . but, more than that. At the back of the house and gardens there are ten acres of untouched hillside and heath. My husband always wanted it left like that . . . he was so fond of and sympathetic towards all wild life . . . plants and animals. Would you care to?'

'Well, I take that very kindly, ma'am. You say when and I'll be there. I've rented Rose Cottage so I can walk over.'

'Yes, I know. News travels fast in the country. It's a nice cottage, and with a lovely view. Come tomorrow. And what's more you can always feel free to go up there and see what you can find.'

'You're kindness itself, ma'am. Well,' he stood up, 'I left me car up at Selworthy today. So I got a bit of a climb back. See you tomorrow.'

She sat there for a while watching him make his way up the combe. She turned away in time to see the tiercel winging fast and low over the shore breakers towards the point. Just before he reached it he called and then rose with strong wing beats into the face of the wind and disappeared round the edge of the cliff fall. As he disappeared she nodded her head. Four days before she had walked the shingle beach at dead low water and partly rounded the point where, after sitting patiently for an hour, she had seen the falcon rise on a small, clearly back-sloping ledge, fan her wings momentarily, almost in cormorant fashion, and then launch herself into flight. The nest site had been chosen cleverly. There would be few people who would mark it. And it all depended on what kind of people they were whether the birds brought off their brood or not. One thing a nest robber would have to be, she knew, was a competent rock climber. Early morning and late evening were the danger times for the birds. She sighed and stood up to walk back to her car. From far up the combe now Alfie Grey turned and waved to her and she waved back. A nice man . . . but something a bit odd about him. Nice odd, or nasty odd, she wondered, and then sighed. So difficult to tell these days, so difficult. When she was young you blushed if you told a lie. Today the young of both sexes could be brazen and yet carry it off with such charm and conviction.

4

Maurice Kirkman leaned over the stern rail of the cross-Channel ferry and, without a trace of nostalgia or regret, watched the coast drop slowly into the late evening haze of the skyline. Good-bye old England . . . Welcome Katje and a new life. A real, new start . . . own garage, own boss, a boy for you and a girl for me . . . Oh, what a happy family we shall be. Or something like that it went, he recalled. And below on the car deck, the second-hand Volvo he had bought. A bargain and, since he was going Continental, why bother with a British car? Trouble with spares and nobody wanting to know . . . Oh, yes . . . life was taking on a rosy tint, the sun rising on a new life. Except at the moment it was setting, glowing like a great red orange, into a bank of dark clouds in the West.

He went below and had a couple of beers and a plate of sandwiches. The boat got in late at Ostend. He'd take a kip in the saloon and then, when she docked, he would be fresh for the drive from Ostend up to Amsterdam. Always take the long way round, maxim one, for beginners who had never seen the remains of a chum blown up on a land mine. Not a nice sight.

Funny business, all this political stuff, and — if you looked at it straight — it was all kid's stuff. Juvenile antics — not a home-grown phrase of his own, but the echo from some school teacher in his distant past. If they really wanted to do Sir Anthony Swale in, why not, as it were, do it to his face? Ring the door bell of the flat, walk in, a couple of shots and walk out again. Just as safe as any other way. No, they always seemed to like to dress it up . . . false moustaches, things that weren't what they seemed and most of all, he supposed, the lovely gory headlines in the morning papers. Look, see what we done, see what we can do . . . so all you others be good boys and girls and toe the party line.

Funny lot, people. Say what you like, you could never read 'em true. Why the hell did Sir Anthony take to working for the other side? Got everything . . . so what? Well, perhaps when you did, then you went for something most others didn't have the guts or devil to attempt. Forbidden fruit . . . and, he grinned to himself, he'd take odds that if the truth could ever be known then Eve had only just beaten Adam at grabbing the rosy apple . . . a nice juicy pippin . . .

He walked down the starboard side, a

coldish westerly breeze flapping the skirts of his raincoat. Few people about and most of them on the port side out of the wind. And of course, a chap should always have a good reason for his actions. My God, they were good days in the army . . . Northern Ireland gave a man scope, and a lot went on that never made the headlines . . . He turned his coat collar up about his neck, shivered a little, and then settled down into his coat and leaned over the rail watching the night thicken across the water and waiting for it to happen. He chuckled to himself. They must have thought he still had the egg round his mouth. Well, the money was safe. He'd checked that with Katje. But they wouldn't be worrying about the money. They would be worrying about a mouth to shut for ever. His. Couldn't blame them. Might have done the same in their place.

Come on, lads, he thought. The scene's all set. Darkness enough. This little bit of the deck free of all but himself. And, from what he had been able to piece together since leaving port, more likely two than one. The one he had already spotted. The wind rose suddenly, a sharp burst of squall and a thin, driving curtain of brief rain. Tall chap, darkie like, touch of the tar brush there somewhere. And now he saw the other . . . short, thin, weasel . . . Christ, the worst kind. Big boys were always slow, so slow sometimes that it dammed near amounted to politeness — *Sorry chum, but kindly turn round slowly while I put the pretty little knife into your guts. Nothing personal of course.* The kind the Paras always turned down. Weasel was the one. A dear, little cuddly number, big smile, milk of human kindness wet on his lips, and knowing to an inch just the place to put the knife between the ribs while the other clamped hand over your mouth and lifted . . . Oh dear, oh dear — did I hear something go splash? Some fool happy dolphin showing off, or the Loch Ness monster going twice round the British Isles for a constitutional. Keep fit, keep happy. Well, well, and here they were . . . Not another soul in sight. All saloon and bar bound.

He turned as they moved and acted before they could. They both had knives and so hampered one another. More rehearsal needed. Time spent on reconnaissance is seldom wasted . . . ditto a mock-up rehearsal.

He took the up-raised hand of Weasel, twisted it to hear the sinews crack and the knife fall as he dropped almost to one knee and drew the man over his shoulder, clear of the rails into the sea with a lovely, obliging momentum supplied by the co-operative victim and, as he rose, he went in under the now somewhat startled other man's guard and kneed him viciously in the genitals with a force that made him gasp with almost the same noise and throwing back of head and mouth opening that comes to some at the supreme moment of love-making. And in that moment of surrogate ecstasy he took the man's right arm, wrist and armpit hold, half dropped and spun him like a catherine wheel over the rail as a burst of high wind and rain came in on cue from the gentleman above or below — according to your feelings in the matter, he told himself — who was in charge of the *mise en scène*.

He drove off the ferry at Ostend, smiling, a thin little whistle pursing his lips, and thought of the coming night when he would be in Amsterdam. The double room already booked by Katje. A bath, maybe shared . . . anyway, warmth and love, the smell of Floris's *Stephanotis* sweetening the air as she walked, bath robe ungirdled, her warm flesh enticing him with brief and random exposures. God in His Heaven . . . forgive him but what could you do in a world that had such people as himself in it? You were marked for what you were to be long before you was even a gleam in your father's eye.

They met at Sotheby's in Bond Street, were there a little over half an hour, then went by taxi to the Savoy Hotel for lunch. Sir Anthony was in one of his easy-going, almost over-friendly moods during which, though he could only give Richard Crane a few years, he treated him in near to the same manner he would have used to a grown-up son. He wanted all the news from Swale Place, and it was only when he had been satisfied that Crane had the chance to ask him about his own health.

'Oh, you know these specialists. Each one has his pet hobby horse. This was a new chap and, I must say, either he or someone for him had done their homework on me. Makes a good impression you know. A few minutes art talk . . . fairly well researched but no more natural to him than if my gardener had suddenly begun to talk about *À la Recherche du Temps Perdu* . . . and then strip down and get on the couch . . . blood pressure and all the ritual. Sometimes I think it is practically all ritual. Friend of mine once hurt his ankle stepping out of a cab. The Harley Street savants treated him for a pulled tendon. Dissatisfied after three months he went to an osteopath who took one feel and said he'd got a broken something-or-other bone . . . Never trust experts. They don't like dealing in the commonplace things. It's the same with the big London dealers. They pick up something . . . can't positively identify it but instead of being honest they come up with something like — School of Bill Jones of Vienna, late 15th Century, or a set of painted panels in the Ottoman Rococo style, when some — the real rascals — know very well that the Ottoman Rococo stylist is alive and well and living in Nassington Road, Hampstead.'

Crane laughed. 'Well, you're in good form, Sir Anthony. Your quack must have hit the nail on the head for a change.'

'Very true. I feel good. We'll have a couple more days looking round up here and then we'll drive down to Swale Place. I could do with some fishing and shooting.' He fingered his brandy glass for a moment or two and then, in a very changed voice, went on, 'There's something I'd like to ask you to do for me — ' He laughed. 'Oh, nothing very difficult, and anyway it would only be when we were together.'

'I'll do anything I can, of course. What is it?'

'Well, doctor's advice and all that. But they tell me — which I've known for years of course — that I smoke too much. I've done and do a lot of other things too much. They are always, of course, as the Devil has arranged, the nice, exciting and the comforting things of life. During the day it's cigarettes. At night . . . well, cigars. Tried a pipe once or twice but could never get on with it. However — and this is between ourselves — ' He burst into laughter and, shaking his head, went on, 'For God's sake don't look so solemn. It's only that — when we're together — and you see me reach for my cigarette case then you just say — *Que vous y réfléchissiez, monsieur.* That will help me to cut down. You know, down in the store room, working, I just take the damn things without knowing I do it. Wouldn't ask you to do this, but you're a dear chap, and the old quack was pretty forthright about it. You see . . . '

For a moment or two there was a note in his employer's voice which was almost pleading and which strangely touched Crane.

' . . . I'm so bloody awful at disciplining myself over some things. And I've got a hell of a lot to do yet with the collection. The chief thing . . . and I don't know whether I'll be able to swing it, but there's a chance . . . is that I want to give the bulk of it to the nation in my own lifetime and — ' He grinned with

134

a sudden impishness which touched Crane, ' — and in return make some sort of deal over Swale Place and the estate so that my nephew and those after him could hold it à perpète.' He was silent, musing for a moment or two. 'I think it would work, you know. Yes, I think it might. There's a lot I could give for the favour . . . a hell of a bloody lot. But it's all going to take time. Anyway, whenever we're alone and you see me reach for a cigarette . . . just let me have it like my old French governess used to . . . réfléche, chéri, réfléche . . . He leaned back and laughed and added, 'My goodness — there was a woman. Not that I knew it at the time, but later when I looked at the photographs of myself with her as a child. A gorgeous piece. And I wouldn't be surprised if my father didn't think so and act on it.'

* * *

Maurice drove up from Rotterdam to Amsterdam, taking his time because he knew that otherwise when he arrived Katje would be at work and he did not want it that way . . . No, he had written and told her all about it. The way he wanted it. Mr and Mrs Kirkman, a suite booked at the hotel *De l'Europe* by Katje, and Katje from six o'clock

135

onwards — even though it was a day when the shop kept open until half-past eight — waiting for him, and the way she would be, he knew, needing no words of stage management from him because this was now, after his many visits, a ritual between them. The thought of it stirred him, made him tauten his body muscles as though he were contracting himself against the repeated onslaughts of a cold wind.

Marvellous, marvellous, he kept saying to himself, and to avoid arriving too early he made detours, going west to Utrecht and Hilversum and then, because he had been of the same Corps as those many who had jumped and breathed their last there, another detour out to Arnhem and then eventually back via Apeldoorn . . . and the more he saw of the country, the more he liked it, and only a few times, not so many that you could not have counted them on the fingers of one hand, did he give a thought to the two men who had gone into the sea or the immaculate dark green Rolls-Royce that carried instant and devastating destruction in its body.

At half-past six he was at the hotel, car parked and a page boy taking his case and leading him — not one much given to poetic feeling but this time wrought to the pitch by the fierce longing that had carried him through the last weeks with confidence and strong resolve, and to hell with the rest of the world. He signed in and followed the page boy to the lift. Excitement was running high in him. Nothing in the world existed except Katje and the rosy future they were to share.

When they got to the room door, he gave the boy a tip and was thanked with a bow of the head and a pleasant smile. The boy slipped the key into the door lock and then without turning it stood back and walked away.

Maurice Kirkman opened the door and went in carrying his case. He switched the lights on and knew at once that she was not there. The branch of the service he had been in taught its members to use their eyes and common 'savvy'. He knew at once that she was not there . . . should have known down in the reception hall because the room key had been hanging on its hook behind the desk.

He stood there and swore aloud with disappointment. But guessed the trouble. That bloody shop. One of the other assistants had gone ill or something and Katje had not been able to get away. Well, sod that. A few more days and she would never have need to go and work in any shop for the rest of her life.

He checked through the bedroom and the

bathroom and then picked up the telephone and called the shop. The girl who answered was known to him quite well because she with her boy friend had now and then made a foursome for excursions and dances with himself and Katje.

He said, 'Helda — this is Maurice Kirkman here. Can I speak to Katje?'

'Hullo, Maurice. Nice to talk with you again. But is Katje not with you? For two days we think here that is what she does. She takes part of her holiday to be with you.'

'Oh, Gawd — there must be some bloody mix-up. Do you have her telephone number at her lodgings?'

'Yes, I give you.'

She gave him the number and he wrote it down. He called the desk and got them to ring the number for him.

A man answered, picked up at once that he was talking to an Englishman and said, 'Mynheer is English? I was interpreter with the good English boys during the — '

Unable to hold his sharpness, Kirkman said, 'Yes, yes, another time if you please, mynheer. Could I speak with Katje Steen-swaard, please?'

'Ah, sorry to disappoint. But she is left two days ago.'

'Left — to go where?'

'For good. She is paying up all correct. And she goes. Where to who can say?'

'Thank you.'

He put down the receiver and then went over to the drinks dispenser which stood just inside the main doorway. He opened three of the miniature bottles of whisky into a large glass, filled it with ice and then went back and sat on the edge of the large double bed. He knew what had happened and what was happening.

The next day confirmed everything. No money of his had been deposited at the bank, either in his name or Katje's. He drove three hours to the village where she had always been promising to take him to see her parents. A gentle priest who spoke good English assured him that no family called Steenswaard had ever lived there. Maurice Kirkman gave him ten guilders for his poor box and thought . . . let the poor look after the bleedin' poor.

Then as he drove away he began to laugh. First those sodding pair of Tweedledum and Tweedledees with bloody Russian snow on their boots . . . and, can you beat it, chum? I tell you this is one for the Sergeants' Mess, a smooth-assed, plump-titted, gorgeous piece of Dutch delight pulls as neat a little operation as you could imagine never happening to you. Well, well ... Good-bye Piccadilly ... Farewell Leicester Square ... it's a long long way to Tipperary ... But, by God, some bugger's going to pay — even if it ain't the one that owes the money.

⋆ ⋆ ⋆

They motored down to the West Country through a late Spring bright sunny morning. Richard Crane drove while his employer sat alongside him, lost it seemed in some reverie whose content now and then brought from him an occasional subdued grunt as though he were pursuing some inner dialogue with an *alter ego* and, a little surprisingly, was finding much agreement between them.

The man, of course, Crane told himself ... half lost in the pleasure of driving the car which moved like some gentle monster, obedient to the lightest whim of the master hand ... yes, the man himself was two men. He knew one intimately ... the man whose hand moved out and touched the smooth turn of a piece of marble, the acorn-brown bronze of some nereid's lovely rump ... the man who had — and the instinctive wisdom was rare — the gift of almost instant discrimination between the faked and the genuine work. It was almost as though — and

the thought was far from new to him — two if
not three men inhabited the tall, elegant body
and shared the view of life seen from the
dark-pupilled eyes. One was the hard-
drinking, hot-lusting millionaire with a
hundred *droits de seigneur* appended to his
birth certificate. The second . . . well, that
was the one he drove now — a relaxed and, if
he read him right, a silently self-pitying being
knowing that he who had had his lines so
rightly laid in pleasant places at first now
found them all in disarray. Perhaps something, with time, might be saved or restored
to his marriage. He himself, for all his feelings
for her, and knowing she would never leave
him, could hope so. Perhaps the years would
bring them a soothing and meditative calm.
Nothing though, he felt, could ever quench
the basic lust for and instinctive passion to
possess that which took his connoisseur's eyes
or roused his sensual pulse by the display of a
woman's beauty.

From the corner of his eye as they began
the approach of the M4 to the M5 motorway
to take them westwards he saw his employer's
right hand slip into his pocket and pull out a
gold cigarette case. The habit he knew was
deeply settled in him. At this moment he was
probably unaware of his own movements. The
case was flicked open, a cigarette taken, and

the case then shut. Deliberately he let him follow the ritual of years of smoking, hoping that he would come to the memory of his self-pledging.

Sir Anthony tapped the end of the cigarette against the tooled face of the case, then put the cigarette in his mouth and reached out towards the dashboard lighter to push it home. As he did so, and before he could touch the lighter, Crane said pleasantly, '*Que vous y réfléchissiez, monsieur . . .* '

Sir Anthony jerked his head towards him, coming sharply out of his reverie and for a moment his face framed the lines of rising resentment. Then he suddenly smiled and said, 'Thank you, Richard. Thank you. Well . . . If I can't have my usual dose of narcotic let's have some music.'

He put his cigarette case back into his pocket and switched on the radio, fiddled for a while until he found some light music to his taste and then slumped back comfortably in his seat.

They drove then to the accompaniment of light music until they left the motorway at Bridgwater and took the Minehead road. After a mile or so Sir Anthony said, 'All right. You've done your share of driving. I'll take over the last stage. Not exactly a fair division, but an employer must have some privileges.'

142

They both got out to change seats, but while Richard Crane walked around the car's forward part to make the changeover Sir Anthony walked around the rear of the car. As he slid into the driving seat he had a lighted cigarette in his mouth. Adjusting his driving safety belt, he grinned and said, 'Let that be a lesson to you in dealing with addicts. There is so often guile behind their courtesy. And don't think I'm surrendering my cigarette lighter.'

Crane smiled. 'For a beginning I think you've done pretty good, sir. That's the first since London. You could perhaps enter it in the game book — *one Piccadilly Number One, low flying, snap shot . . .* '

'Perhaps so. But I wonder which is easier — moderation or total abstinence?'

'Everyone has a free choice — but it could be that if you choose moderation isn't it a bit like a man at confession saying, 'Father, I have sinned but such small sins it would be a waste of your time to bother you with them.''

To his surprise Sir Anthony jerked his head round swiftly, his eyes holding him full face, sudden anger showing as he said, 'I find that kind of remark in bad taste.'

'Then I'm sorry you do — and I apologize.'

Crane spoke firmly, knowing that he had hit the wayward vein of religious sensitivity in his employer. He had met it before but even so he had never been able to prejudge what kind of remark would start Sir Anthony into a reaction that had all the appearance of anger, true, but uncannily, too, gave the feeling that fear lay behind it.

It had happened only rarely in their acquaintanceship . . . this sudden magnesium flare of passion, but each time it had, he had always been left after a while with a feeling that somewhere . . . deep down . . . the man was disturbed and discontented, almost as though he were harbouring some great sin and unable to seek absolution because the act of confession was denied to him. Quite frankly, he sometimes felt that there could be some onset of mental disorder in the man, brief like summer lightning, but to him while it so shortly endured a source of great terror.

Five minutes later as they drove Sir Anthony turned to him and with a warm, disarming smile said, 'Sorry, Richard — sometimes I get a bit edgy. Now tell me . . . I was thinking about that Cornelius Springer and the Marguerita Pillini. We haven't got much nineteenth-century European stuff . . . paintings, drawings and water colours. Some of them are charming, too. I think we should go for them. You see, it's always been my wish to diversify . . . not necessarily a bit

144

of everything, but representative groupings. There's no fun in sticking in one groove . . . '

★ ★ ★

Alfie Grey saw them arrive. He was sitting on the tump of an old ant-hill in the rough meadow at the top of Mrs Winslade's land which for a certain part of its perimeter marched with the Swale estate. The day before he had taken tea with Mrs Winslade . . . silver teapot, sensibly not too thinly sliced bread and butter (for his benefit, he guessed — that was one nice thing about the nice rich: they thought about others — if they happened to like them. God help you if they didn't) and a lot of easy talk on his part, a great deal of it not strictly true but funny and sometimes a little cheeky which made her laugh, as he knew it would. Women were all the same, sisters under the skin, and just a matter of handling. A man who didn't have the born knack or lacking that didn't take the trouble to learn it . . . well, he'd get nowhere.

She showed him round and he wasn't surprised at how smart and strong a walker she was because he'd seen her going up to Hurlstone Point. No racer but a steady plodder. And he'd found her a bundle of things to take back home and look up in some book she said she had in the library. Sedges, plenty of them on the wet top ... *Carex divulsa* and *vulpina* — just flowering. And there was a bit of marshy ground full of interest ... specially as he found her a little patch of sundews ... *Drosera anglica* as well as *rolundifolia*. Not in flower, but for her to keep her eye on when June and July turned up.

And before she had walked off home, she had said to him, 'I'm so glad I came up here with you. It's always been a favourite place of mine, but I'd no idea there was so much right under my nose that I'd never seen. My husband loved it, too. You'd have liked him ... '

Which probably he would have done, but from the things he'd heard in pub talk on his wanderings around there were a lot of things he wouldn't have liked about him. And which made it odd, because sitting up here now and watching the big Rolls ride up the long drive to Swale Place there were a lot of things about Sir Anthony which, purely on hearsay from the same public sources, he didn't like ... things stretching from wife-beating to whoring ... hard bargaining and no second chance if you did something to put him out while you worked for him ... dear, oh dear. Not nice.

Well, tonight he would give Sir John a ring and tell him that the target was up on the range again and see if there was any special instruction. You never knew with them. If they said ring this number every other night, reversed charges — then you did — and not from Dunster, either. Never operate too close to your own doorstep. The world was full of curious eyes. Always you had to do it from a public call box and there were times when someone waiting could give the dirty look and the hurry-up fist banging on the glass. The telephone in his cottage brought him incoming calls — but unless it was dead urgent all calls to his employers were made from a public call box. Sensible, but a damned nuisance. Impatient buggers some human beings. Which was natural. He got near to it himself now and then.

When he rang Sir John Warboys that evening from a telephone box just off the Minehead promenade giving him a fragmentary view of the sea, sullen grey rollers sweeping in and a few staunchily determined early holiday makers taking their evening walk, mackintoshed and heads down against the onshore wind, he was told to go ahead as soon as he could. But he was not to do it from any viewpoint on private property where he was known to the owner or the owner's servants.

In addition — and he had had this condition laid down on other jobs — once he had dealt with Sir Anthony he was to remain in his cottage for, at least, another two weeks before leaving — but his rifle would be collected from him immediately the job was done. Very particular they were . . . proper gentlemen . . . all for Queen and country and the safety of the realm.

He came out of the box sighing. Sir John was right, of course. Common-sense — but it did make things harder and meant that it might be some time before he got a cast-iron chance to make a successful job of the shooting. Still . . . it wasn't as though he didn't get paid handsomely for waiting time, and his dear wife wouldn't be missing him. Nice not to have him underfoot for a change. Proper Darby and Joan they were together but . . . well, absence made the heart grow fonder.

⋆ ⋆ ⋆

After dinner they took their coffee in the small conservatory beyond the dining room, with one of the windows open to give them the evening garden scents and the smell of recently mown lawns. Once an early moth came blundering in and he got up, trapped it eventually with his folded handkerchief, and went out on to the veranda to release it. As he came back he grinned at her and said, 'Useless pieces of information litter our lives. What's the difference between a butterfly and a moth?'

'I've no idea . . . ' She smiled at him, and the smile was genuine. This is what he could achieve when he wished or perhaps at times without such deliberation . . . a personality change. And one so welcome, even though she knew it would never last. Warm, charming, amusing and, sometimes, a little pathetic as though he were suing for sympathy.

'Nearly all butterflies sit with their wings raised above their backs — but the great majority of moths rest with their wings outspread or wrapped closely around their body.'

'I never knew.'

'Well, it's not vital information.'

He came and sat down, took out a cigar and began to prepare it with the slow and expert deliberation of a man who curbs his approach to coming pleasure knowing that anticipation is the zest that heightens all soon to be savoured delights. Looking at her now he acknowledged without any great emotional stir that had he had the sense and the self-discipline to have elevated his feelings for her above all others . . . Aye, worshipped her and been true, then the run of his days and the tangles so cast about him might all have been smoothed away. He laughed silently to himself. What a hope. Old Nick had tempted him, but not with any crude delights . . . money or women. Oh, no . . . but with a lust for the works of the world's great artists . . . be they saints or sinners, they were above all human constraints. By his deep worship of their works so became he endowed with some portion of their creators' immunity . . . their remoteness from ordinary men. And might it not be that the good Lord kept a soft spot in His heart for the sinners amongst them . . . including himself. He smiled at the thought.

That night he went to her room and was kind and gentle and they enjoyed one another, though even as they did he knew that it could never last for this was only what his present mood made acceptable.

* * *

The idea came to Maurice Kirkman as he lay in bed in the very early morning cradled

150

between dying sleep and rising wakefulness. He rolled over from lying flat on his stomach and went suddenly from slowly receding sleep to wide awakefulness.

Aloud, he said, 'You bloody fool, Maurie boy. You bloody, bloody fool . . . '

And so he was, but at least he now told himself — with a little need for self-justification — that was not to be surprised at seeing that, at this moment, he by rights should have had Katje in bed with him, all warm and dairy fresh, and the whole world of honest work and good profits as a self-employed man waiting for him to open it up like a Christmas hamper — a thing he'd never, of course, had in his life but knew all about because his garage boss used to send small ones to his best customers and he, Maurice Kirkman, did the deliveries.

All right . . . he'd lost Katje, but there were others in the world, and if the major part of his capital had now gone . . . well, he was still young and life was there stuffed full of all sorts of opportunities from dead honest ones right up through all the shades of righteousness and so on to the golden crests of criminal ingenuity. Not that this first thought showed the way. But it was a morale booster . . . and every man needed that when the going was tough. Like his old sergeant used to say in the Paras at bayonet drill with the long line of stuffed dummies waiting . . . *in, twist, out, and on . . . keep it in yer mind lads . . . they've all had yer girls, yer wives, yer mothers and old grandma if she's still at home . . .* Yes, that was it. Get your own back. That done you'd feel a different man. He still had some money, a car, and the world was his oyster . . . and one thing for sure — he wasn't going to hang around sobbing his heart out. He was on his own and all life was waiting out there, still up for grabs — but never again would he be fooled by any woman. From now on they were strictly second-hand, second-class citizens.

He got up, shaved and dressed and went down to breakfast. None of your Continental crap of a cup of coffee and two rolls and tiny tubs of fruit flavoured jelly. Coffee and toast and two fried eggs with a thick slice of ham. As he ate he composed the letter in his mind. When he had finished he went into the lounge and wrote his letter on a sheet of hotel writing paper, using his own ball-point pen.

It didn't worry him about the hotel name. By the time it reached England he would be gone, leaving no forwarding address. As he wrote he now and then said under his breath — bastards, bastards — and the picture of Leo Chukolev came into his mind — a

bloody monkey in a rumpled blue suit.
The letter read:

Dear Sir Anthony,
   You won't know who I am, but that's no
matter — except that you'll be able to find
out if you want to, and I don't care a damn
about that. Or about getting paid. I just
want to do those buggers down just like I
been done down but not by them. That's
right, a woman and I got to smash
somebody for it.
   I don't know their name except they're
Ruskies all right, and their money's good.
The money that I got for the job. But the
buggers tried to do me on the Channel
boat and I ditched both of the sods. Not
Chukolev and Popplehov what give me the
thing to fix to your Rolls. Two others. So
— you just take notice of this for it's all
dead true. There's this bomb thing under
your Rolls and the first time you press the
cigarette lighter you and the whole car will
go skyhigh. That's it — there's no more to
say except I hope this gets to you in time.
                              Sincerely

He signed it 'A Wellwisher', put it in an
envelope and addressed it to Sir Anthony at
his London mews flat. He got a stamp at the

desk and dropped the letter into the hotel box. At the hotel kiosk he bought an English paper and then went to the lift. A man and woman got in just ahead of him. As Maurice Kirkman followed them the man standing by the indicator board raised his hand to the floor panel board and said, in English, 'What number?'

'Third floor, please,' Kirkman said. Then, as the man pushed the ascent button, he added, 'Nice of you.'

The woman smiled and he saw now that she was a fine piece of homework even though she was never going to see fifty again. She said, 'We also.'

They rode up to the third floor. When the lift stopped and the doors swung open Kirkman stood back for the woman to leave first. She gave him a little nod of her head in thanks and he thought to himself . . . spirits lightened by the afterglow from the letter he had written . . . that she'd still be a lively number.

They went down the corridor just ahead of him. They passed the door of his room a couple of yards in front of him. As he stopped and began to put his key into the lock there came a small cry of dismay from the woman. He heard her say something in Dutch to the man far too rapidly for him to understand.

The man turned with a shrug of his shoulders and began to walk back towards the lift. As he came level with Kirkman he grinned and said in good English, 'My wife has left her handbag in the breakfast room. Women . . .'

Kirkman laughed. 'Bad luck.'

He turned away and began to fit his key into the door lock. As the key turned and the door began to swing open he felt a sharp stabbing pain in the small of the back. He gave an anguished cry that was half smothered by a hand, coming round from behind him, clamping over his mouth while another slid round his waist on his left side and took the weight of his already sagging body. Through a mist of fast rising, fierce stabbing pain he saw the woman close in on him and, as they helped him through the now open door of his room, he heard her say, 'Such a fine looking young man . . .' and then no more.

★　★　★

Walking the lower fringe of the long top wood which created the gentle slope that ran down to his house and grounds, gun under his arm and — no matter the main run of his thoughts — his senses awake for the first sight of rabbit or wood pigeon — Sir Anthony, in a relaxed frame of mind and for now, at least, untouched by any feeling of self pity, wondered why *they* had let him run free so long. Longer, in fact, than was usual . . . but then perhaps in his case wiser . . . better the devil you know. Well, on the whole, the things he had passed had been seldom material. More usually, and much more useful, it had been some detail of others' private lives . . . the hidden vices, the skeletons in the cupboards of the ambitious and so vulnerable parvenus.

How long ago and how simple and innocuous the beginning had been . . . Just three months after his first election to Parliament . . . and already the party with its eye on him . . . promising material . . . good family and a safe West Country seat. And then, through his own uncontrolled appetite for life's material and aesthetic pleasures, had come the gradual enmeshment. No sudden spider rush as the web shivered to the unwary blunder of victim into the finely spread and almost invisible net. Oh, no . . . pure temptation. A woman and a picture . . . God knows, today he could hardly credit his lustful naïveté. And he still young enough and so full of ambition that his self-confidence seemed impregnable — but only to prove no defence against the twin thrusts of lust and longing — firstly, the body of a woman against whom one breath of scandal reaching her husband's ears would have closed every avenue in public life to him for ever, and secondly since already his aesthetic senses rivalled those of his body, an Attic red-figure cup by the Antiphon Painter . . . 490 B.C. One inconstant and the other constant joy. And then, later, had come the simplest of requests which took his compliance for granted.

A voice from his right said, 'Good morning, Sir Anthony.'

He half-turned, knowing from whom it came, welcoming the West Country accent.

'Good morning, Steve. What are you after? Pigeons?' The youth had a shotgun under one arm and a sack thrown over his shoulder.

'Well, if I get a chance, yes. But I'm setting rabbit snares. They're playing hell with the young corn in the top field.' The youth paused, grinned, and then went on, 'I'm glad I met you, Sir Anthony. It's the Rugger Club dance next week. I know you don't go but you usually buy a couple of tickets. All in a good cause . . . we're working for a new pavilion.'

'Of course I will. Bring 'em round this evening some time and have a drink and I'll pay you for the tickets.' He grinned. 'Do I have three guesses as to which girl you're taking?'

Steve laughed. 'No need to guess, sir. If I was taking any other life wouldn't be worth living. We're making up a party . . . six or eight of us. Going to hire a car and draw lots for who stays teetotal to drive. We do that every year. No escape, not even if you have already done it the year before.'

'You should hire a chauffeur.'

'Maybe — but the car hire is enough. A chauffeur would cramp our style too.'

'Well . . . come along this evening with the tickets. Lady Swale will be pleased to see you.'

'I will, Sir Anthony. Oh, and by the way, sir . . . there's something you'd like to know seeing as you're interested in that kind of thing '

'What kind of thing?'

'Them falcon birds. Peregrines. Jim Archer — he plays scrum half for our lot and lives up at Selworthy. He's pretty sure that a pair of peregrines are nesting somewhere on Hurlstone Point.'

'Oh, well that *is* interesting. I must go and have a look at them.'

Walking on, Sir Anthony thought . . . that's what I wanted — a son. A young man like that . . . Though would it have made any difference to the other things . . . to the way things were with his wife?

He turned aside as he entered a fir plantation and began to walk down an open ride that led to the river and the path back to Swale Place. When he came to the bridge he stopped as he always did to look over the side . . . as he had looked far back in his father's day. The dark shape of a trout slid smoothly away from foraging the main channel and disappeared into a patch of downstream weeds. Elbows on the bridge rail, chin cupped in his hands, he remembered the time he had, as a boy, been like this with his father and the closeness of their relationship when they were alone. In company they maintained different roles. But alone his father spoke to him as his years grew and he passed from preparatory school to public school as though he were already a man and — although he knew now that it was a privilege which was far from wise — privy to far more of the darker and seamier sides of life. Now — so many years on and so much more experienced, he knew that it had been unwise of his father . . . too much and too soon. Warning him of temptations and follies still far distant had merely made him impatient for their arrival.

He spat into the water, a ritual, and went on to the house. Finding his wife in the hall arranging flowers he moved to her and gave her a kiss on the side of the cheek and then said, 'Young Stephen Black's coming in this evening for a drink and to sell me tickets for the Rugby dance.' He grinned. 'I don't suppose you'd care to go?'

'I would if you really wanted to.'

'Well, you're safe. I don't. But I like the lad . . . and I don't have to tell you why. There was never anything we could do about it. But, God, it would have been nice to have had a son, and one with a bit of wildness and mischief in him. Anyway, I'm thinking of giving him a surprise.'

She smiled. 'A nice one, I hope.'

'Of course. They hire a car, you know, to take themselves and their girls to the dance. They draw lots and one unlucky chap has to stay sober. I thought I'd let them have the Rolls. I don't see why they shouldn't have it and the chap who's unlucky in the draw can drive it. And he can bring it back here the next morning. What do you think?'

She put out a hand and touched his arm, warming to him and yet at the same time wondering how he could be so many different persons. She said, 'I think it's a good idea and very generous of you. I suppose it's all right for them to drive it? I mean — '

'Good Lord, my love. You're way behind

the times. In nineteen-hundred-and-forty chaps their age were flying Spitfires in the Battle of Britain.'

★ ★ ★

They lay together in the hay on the top floor of the old barn that stood in the corner of a field which was backed by a tall stand of pines and in the front commanded a view down the valley slope to the distant brook and the small notch of sea visible beyond Minehead. Although Spring still held sway the nights were getting warmer and today was the first time they had used the old barn this year.

They had made love, if not fully, then liberally within what were now precisely limited boundaries of conjoining and caressing. Her head cradled on his shoulder, their hands moved in slow and intimate caresses and, although short of true and loving full licence, far enough now within the extended limits of their passion to leave them both so deeply spent that there were times when they lay together in half sleep, half wakefulness.

She said drowsily, 'You seem to get on with him. But my Dad don't. But maybe that's because they're two of a kind. Always looking to be done down. And if someone does them a good turn or offers too good a deal — then they're looking for the catch in it all. I can't say I like him. His eyes go over you in that way.'

'What way?'

'You know what I mean.'

He laughed. "Course I do ... like this ... ?' His right hand moved over her and she would have twisted away from him only he held her tightly and, as he put his lips to hers, he felt her relax and lie in his arms without anxiety or struggle, and found the surge of desire rising in him as her fingers tightened on the back of his neck and her mouth slowly opened, velvet-lipped and eager for the warmth and the masterfulness of his maleness. They lay locked together without movement, holding each other, while from outside in the growing dusk came the bleating of the Spring lambs, the lyrical evensong of a blackbird in the briar brake behind the barn, and then distantly the first melancholy call of a barn owl.

When their embrace slowly slackened and she half-rolled from him and through the open loft door saw the slowly reddening sky in the west as the sun, already hidden by the far valley side, dropped seaward, she sighed and found the sigh running rapidly through her body until her shoulders and arms began to tauten and quiver with the surge of emotional and physical current that flooded through her.

She said with slow deliberation and knowing that what she was going to demand was as much for herself as for him, as much for the easing of her mind and body's impatience as his, and knowing, too, that the laying down of conditions was no more than a formality than any imposing of a trial which he might or might not overcome, 'You've got to drive, haven't you? For the Rugger do.'

'Yes. Bugger it.' He grinned.

'So you've got to keep sober?'

'True — but I've had a fair run without doing it. Anyway, like I told you . . . Sir Anthony's letting us have the Rolls. That's something to keep sober for. There's not much a man wouldn't give up something or other for if the incentive is strong enough. We don't have to take the car straight back . . . drive along to Countisbury and see the dawn come up like thunder from China cross the bay . . . or whatever it was.'

'What was?'

'Never mind. But what are you getting at?'

'You — and staying sober. Not drinking. You can do that?'

'Sure — most of the other chaps have all

done it in their turn. Anyway I'll have you alongside me.'

She was silent for a moment and then she put out a hand and laid it against his cheek and said gently, 'If you did something to please me . . . well, then, I'd do anything you asked . . . *anything* to please you.'

'Anything?'

She looked straight at him with only the smallest sketch of a smile beginning to touch her lips and repeated, 'Yes . . . anything. Though I'd have to go on the — '

He reached for her right hand, saying. 'There's no need to say any more. I'd do anything for you . . . ' He grinned. 'Well, except jump off a cliff. So what do you want?'

She said, 'Hold out your right hand.'

He did so, with his fingers spread wide. She touched his first two fingers which were brown with the nicotine that came from his smoking.

With a slow, almost ashamed motion which touched her deeply, he slowly withdrew his hand from her hold, saying, 'Oh, I see . . . Well, I suppose you're right. Ma's always on at me. But Dad doesn't mind . . . ' He grinned. 'He says . . . No matter what you give up there's always something left that'll do for you in the end . . . like a bus or a bomb.'

'You'd like to sleep with me properly, wouldn't you?'

'Of course . . . '

'I'd like it, too, and I'd make it quite safe. But I'm not asking you to give up smoking as a sort of price for it. If things were right we could do it now . . . ' She suddenly giggled. 'Oh, dear . . . if you could see your face. It's not all that serious. I'm not asking you to go out and kill some dragon and — '

He suddenly moved to her and forced her back from her sitting position to the ground, spread her full length, her arms pinned down, his body on her and then he lowered his head and took her lips. As she relaxed under him he let her arms go free and felt them come round him.

Ten minutes later, the dusk purpling the sky, a car's headlights glow-worming its way up the valley, and the first call of a barn owl filling the air with the mellow mournfulness of its evening complaint, he rolled from her. Lying on his back and staring at the web-shrouded rafters of the barn, he said, 'You know I'll do it. But in my own way and time. I got to do the driving for the Rugger Ball — that means ease right down on the drink. Fair enough. But I don't want to have to lay off the cigarettes as well. They go from the next day onwards. I'll do it, all right.

You'll see.' He suddenly laughed. 'My goodness, too. I've just thought of something. I'll save quite a bit of money, won't I?'

* * *

Janice Burton opened the mews flat door with her key and, as it swung after her, bent down and picked up the pile of letters which lay in the wire frame container under the letter box mouth.

Shuffling them into a tidy bundle she went through into the sitting room and put the pile on the gate-legged table by the window which overlooked the mews lane. A chauffeur backed a car out of the garage opposite and then, as he got out of the car to close the garage doors before driving off, looked up and saw her. With a grin he blew her a kiss which she acknowledged with a brief wave of her hand — thinking to herself that, on the whole, you didn't meet many of them that didn't think they were God's gift to women whereas most of them weren't worth wasting a sheet of fancy wrapping paper on to pack them up — leave alone wasting money on stamps to send them off. Still . . . just a few odd ones broke the rule. Like Frankie Tolly — a no-gooder if there ever was one, but all fun and excitement, overcharged and generous with everything he had. The kind a girl needed for a while . . . once in a lifetime . . . before settling down.

Funny really because he was a bit like Sir Anthony — take away the money and position. Up to a point they had a lot in common, but beyond that point . . . well, Frankie was left trailing. Nothing solid. Into this and out of that. She smiled to herself as she thought of the reaction of her father the first time — and the only time — she had taken him home. Her father had said later — *You're of age, you do what you want and you pick your own friends. But understand this — bring that fellow here again and I'll kick him out. For God's sake — don't you know a bad penny when you see one?* Yet the only time Sir Anthony had met her father — he had driven her home on a wild and wet evening — he had been all over him. Sir Anthony Swale, Bart. Frankie Tolly. Brothers under the skin. Neither of them fooled her — but they were both fun in bed and out, and, since the bomb could go off any moment, fun was the in-thing. Mind you, working for Sir Anthony was also fun. Chiefly she dealt with all the documentary side of his art dealings . . . customs clearance certificates and sucking up to officials, usually minor, of all nations who were — until firmly disillusioned — far more interested in her than they ever could have been in Venus de Milo or a painted smile from *La Gioconda*.

Sometimes she helped out in constituency matters . . . dreary days in Yorkshire wearing a big smile and a bigger rosette and his agent always bum-pinching and itching to get her into bed. Without luck. Not that that applied to Sir Anthony. For him she made not infrequent exceptions. But for her — and always to be a mystery why — there was only one person and that was Frankie . . . Frankie who had wiped clear the memory of all the others before him. Well, if not clear, smudged them so that they were soon so amorphous that they never troubled her memory.

She went through the pile of letters, opening them all except those which were marked *Private* or *Confidential*. The ones she opened were all of little importance and which she knew Sir Anthony could deal with over the telephone to her after the week-end. There were three letters marked *Confidential* and one marked *Private*. The one marked *Private* bore a Netherlands stamp and was addressed in blue ink in a rough hand. The others were typewritten.

Half an hour later a car horn sounded outside the flat. Going to the window she saw him waiting for her, in a car she had never seen before, but that was no surprise since he did a bit of dealing when he got the chance and was always switching cars. He gave her a wave and made his 'shall I come up sign'. She knew what that would mean and felt it would be good to have it to look forward to . . . besides Frankie was always much better and attentive company the longer he was kept waiting. She shook her head and he grinned and put his thumb to his nose at her.

She picked up the re-directed *Private* and *Confidential* letters to repost to Swale Place and went down to him. Twenty minutes later they were on the M4 heading west. Frankie had a brother who ran a garage on the outskirts of Swindon.

Janice on being told where they were going asked, 'Why are we going down there?'

Frankie grinned, and said, 'A couple of reasons . . . because I haven't seen Syd for some time. Very close we are as brothers. Also this car's about clapped out and he'll let me have another. Also he's got a little bungalow on the river near Cricklade and, being a bachelor, he's none too tidy-like so I said we'd tidy it up for him. 'Course doing that'll make us a bit tired — ' he gave her a big grin, ' — but he's got a nice king-sized bed in which we can rest for a while and listen to the

169

sound of the river running by. Got a thing for rivers, old Syd has. He's a sucker for any house on a river ... desirable riverside property, lovely garden, own moorings, floods twice a year — Spring and Autumn. No fisherman, though.'

She said, 'You're always changing cars. What sort of arrangement do you have with Syd?'

'Arrangement? We're brothers. No arrangement. He's older than me, so I do what he tells me — knowing he'd never land me in real big trouble — and then he gives me a handout. You think the second-hand motor trade is tricky, don't you? Well, Miss Fancy Pants private secretary, so it is — and so is your boss's business. One man one vote. The will of the majority rules.' He snorted and then laughed. 'Know what Syd says, and he knows? The worst people to deal with in his business are the so-called do-gooders. Politicians, parsons and public welfare creeps. They always expect a bigger mark-down than anyone else. We're all equal, of course, but some are ... etcetera ... etcetera.' He put out a hand and ran it down the inside of her leg and laughed as she tried to control the gentle shiver that went through her, flooding up through her body to fountain smoothly across her shoulders and down her arms and, finally, made her spread her fingers wide as though to give freer release to the rich flood of physical sensation that inhabited her body briefly.

He said, 'Nice, ain't it, dear?' Then, as his fingers firmed across the smooth run of her inner thigh, he went on, 'Destiny is the name of the game. The lady's going to have a baby so the boys and girls upstairs get out the dice and have one throw each. Appearance, sex, character, glib or glum, lucky or unlucky, heaven-fingered or devil-touched.' He laughed. 'Some dice with all those sides but the gods never just use six-sided dice. Special ones to keep pace with *homo sapiens* and his quick change acts. But I see . . . ' He shook his head, ' . . . you don't know what the hell I'm talking about. Never mind.'

When they reached his brother's garage, Syd was at a pump serving petrol. He gave them a wave and nodded for them to drive the car into the garage.

As they got out of the car he came in to them, gave Janice a kiss and a hug, and then fisted his brother playfully but solidly against his right shoulder. He grinned and said to Janice, 'All right, love, you know where it is. Here's the flat key.' He fished in his pocket and brought out a key for her which she took and then moved to the stairs which led to his flat over the garage.

He said, when she was gone, 'She's a nice girl, or nicer than most then. Why don't you settle for her?'

'Too soon. And anyway, I don't think she'd want it.'

'They all do sooner or later. Love and marriage they go together like a horse and carriage. And talking of carriages — how long have you had that old passion wagon out there?'

'I don't know. It goes.'

'Blow up in your face one day. Anyway . . . ' he grinned, ' . . . big surprise from Big Brother. Run your heap of junk into the back of the showroom and then pick anything you like from there. Can't have my brother driving round in something a gypsy wouldn't give a second glance at.'

'You mean it?'

'Well, the truth ain't often uttered in these halls, but for once it is. Pick what you want and then get the documents from the office for transfer of ownership. All open and above board this . . . which makes a change for you, no?'

'Maybe, but no surprise. You can even make truth work for you. However, whenever did I enquire into your affairs?'

When Janice came down he was waiting for

172

her with a white Rover 2500. He said, 'Syd asked me to try it out. Said if I like it I could have it. He could use the other for spare parts.'

'Gosh, that's the kind of brother to have.'

'Generous — that's Syd. Runs in the family.'

Just before they reached the riverside bungalow Janice said, 'Oh, hell — I left all Sir Anthony's mail in the car. We'll have to go back for it.'

Frankie, the bungalow with its wide bed two hundred yards ahead — and who cared about the letters anyway? — said, 'Oh, those . . . I asked Syd to put 'em in with the garage stuff this evening. Wouldn't want to keep a Member of Parliament from his complaints mail, would we?' He laughed and, mimicking a strange female voice, went on, ''Dear Sir Anthony . . . I been voting steady for you for years but no more if something isn't done about 'Arry's back. We still ain't no nearer compensation for his back from the fall and now in the winter he seizes up something cruel and sometimes don't come out of it till Spring.''

She laughed and said, 'What did 'Arry fall from?'

'Some say one thing and some another, but most think it was from climbing a tree after forbidden fruit.' He put out a hand and squeezed her thigh. She laughed, and then shook a little with a nervous frisson not so much at the touch but at what it signalled. He smiled to himself and thought there was nothing wrong with life so long as you knew how to handle people . . . keep 'em happy . . . work at it . . . tell a few lies if they fitted. After a time people got fed-up to the eyeballs hearing the real truth about things. Anyway Syd would probably find the letters and stick them in the post. That is unless he meant to do it right away . . . say a little before midnight. Syd never had to use straight words with him — just the gift of the car was enough . . .

Just after midnight the garage caught fire — its cause was never positively identified — and was burnt to the ground. The letters in Frankie's old car were reduced to black and grey dust — amongst them was the last letter ever written by Maurice Kirkman. Frankie, knowing his brother, was unsurprised, but being an honest and honourable man and not wanting to put any strain on his relationship with Janice, he told her of the fire and also said that his brother wanted her to know that her letters with all his had been posted on his way home from the garage before the fire started. After all, no true lover

174

would go out of his way on a mere point of veracity and so risk ending a pleasant relationship . . . and, anyway, Frankie hated to see women upset, no matter what their looks or their age.

★   ★   ★

The first egg had been laid on the 29th March, and by the 2nd April there was a complete clutch of three eggs, clearly marked with red-brown flecks and violet blotches against their white ground. Two days later a cock magpie took one of the eggs as the peregrines flew together at a great height and the tiercel dropped through a thin mist cloud and took the lead bird in an echelon of racing pigeons, released at Land's End and making the sea flight across the Bristol Channel on their way to Cardiff.

From then on the rock ledge eyrie was only briefly left unattended. Although the breeding ledge was high up the face of the rock point it was not by any means a difficult climb to anyone of normal, healthy physique, though the drop should a man slip could be a killing one if that day his luck were out . . . but luck or no luck he would never have come off unscathed.

Very few people knew of them because

man seldom looks up these days . . . not even the high whine of a Concorde makes him stand and stare in wonder any longer. Those who loved them for what they were kept their knowledge to themselves.

Sir Anthony knew they were there. He had discovered them for himself as he walked the high ground above the band of fir trees that marked the highest point of his parkland proper. Walking the higher boundary of the firs, a gun in his arms, he took a snap shot at a pigeon which came over the fir tops fast and low and dropped into a wide area of bramble brake with a crash. After it came the tiercel, the hiss of its half-winged diving stoop loud and so suddenly upon him that Sir Anthony felt the cold frisson of flesh-warning run up his spine and shake his shoulders. He swore aloud at his own shock and the nerve trembling that still lingered in his body. From his high point he watched the bird gain height and head away to the north and east. Though there could be no certainty to it he did not feel it was a Countisbury bird, nor would he have been interested in it had it been, for that area would never have served his purpose. To avoid the law a man must have easy access, stroll like a tourist or botanist, and wait on chance coming at the right moment for taking. He owed a debt of friendship in the

Gulf States. What present can you give a Croesus? Only one that money can't buy. A young peregrine falcon or a tiercel to man . . .

He drove himself one evening in his wife's small car to Bossington, and walked the shingle ridge at low tide, and after an hour he found what he wanted. A pair of jackdaws came round the point and the tiercel dropped on them from a dark-shadowed ledge, scattering them in noisy disarray. This sharp marking of territory was all he wanted to know . . . the rest followed.

5

Alfie knew about the peregrines. One early May afternoon after a visit to take tea with Mrs Winslade he had, just as he turned out on to the Dunster road, seen the baronet's Rolls-Royce a hundred yards ahead of him. Although he was carrying no armament — nor would he until he knew for certain the imminence of the right time and place — he followed the car at a discreet distance and finally found himself turning off the main Porlock road to move down through Bossington towards the sea.

At first he had expected that Sir Anthony would park his car in the tourist car park by the river, but instead the baronet passed it and followed a rough track that took him farther down the river and out on to the fringes of the great sweep of shingle beach.

Alfie slipped his field glasses round his neck, crossed the wooden footbridge over the river and took the downstream path which, at the point where the hillside woods finished, turned sharply upwards to the right to climb the rising headland ground to the top of Hurlstone Point.

Half-way up the path Alfie eased his way through the hedged seaward side of the path and, moving into the bracken and blackberry cover of the sharply falling ground, found an observation point where he could cover the whole stretch of beach from Sir Anthony's parked car away to the left to the grey and rugged rise of the cliff point.

He marked Sir Anthony's laboured walk across the length of shingle beach to the headland and frowned a little as he saw him begin to climb the sharp and often almost precipitous rise of the cliff face. He saw — although he had no precise knowledge of them — the tiercel come off the nesting ledge first and rise high, calling and then circling, and then later the other bird sweep round from the far side of the point just as Sir Anthony reached the nesting ledge and reached out a hand to touch and count the egg clutch. He sighed then for the want of a rifle . . . two hundred yards, with only the faintest adjustment for the in-shore breeze, no bothering with the head or heart region for a certain killing . . . the whine of a bullet and the vicious and high speed drilling of a hit under the left or right shoulder blade . . . no man need get closer than an inner from this distance, but that would serve for, if death were not instantaneous, then the fall would complete the fatal rite. But he knew the kind because his briefing from Sir John Warboys was on this one point — as on all the others — never less than over detailed. The man would be back again. This was the place, here before him was the killing ground. He didn't care a tuppenny damn about the birds or their young. They roused no emotion in him such as he had for grasses and mosses — which, of course, were of greater and older ancestry — but still . . . if a thing couldn't fight back, then live and let live was a good rule of thumb.

A little elated that he had found the killing ground he walked back to his car. As he reached it a police car drew into the small car park. A woman police driver stayed at the wheel as a police sergeant came over to him.

He gave Alfie a formal smile and spoke with a clear flatness of voice which Alfie from experience knew could move from neutrality to distant menace or reluctant acceptance of a to-be-verified truth — and God help you, mister, if it doesn't stand up. He knew that someone must have put them on to him. Not that he cared a damn. Probably some old girl up in the village, sitting at her window watching the world go by and, finding it dull, livening it up a bit with a touch of fantasy.

'I wonder, sir, if you would help us by

answering a few questions. You see a few days ago there was a break-in at the top end of the village and . . . '

Alfie did him the courtesy of listening, but he knew that there probably had never been any break-in. What had happened was that the nervous old lady living on her own had seen him coming and going and, bored with life and needing a little company and self-importance, had dreamt up villainy as a possibility and found it her duty to give the police a ring — and perhaps not for the first time in her declining years. And now here was the nice sergeant who could not afford to neglect the chance that just for once the old girl might be on to something of importance.

' . . . I understand you're often down here and I wondered . . . '

Alfie scarcely bothered to listen to the sergeant's wonderings since they were stereotyped and predictable, but he answered the questions put to him affably, gave his true name and London address as well as that of his hillside cottage, said he was here partly on holiday and partly on business, and that he liked it that way because when you got tired of the one you could switch over to the other, and, no, he couldn't say that he had seen any strangers about because he wouldn't know a stranger from a local, would he — seeing that he was a stranger himself? The sergeant's affability trembled a little for he was a man with a fine ear for the faintest touch of ridicule or, to use his own phrase, 'coming it a shade sarky-like'.

Alfie went on to state his present business and his hobby . . . 'Grasses . . . ' He held up a small bouquet of grasses he had gathered on the way down out of pure habit, and said, touching each exhibit as he spoke, 'That's *Cynodon dactylon* — or Creeping Finger grass and the other's Meadow Fox-tail, or if you want to be botanically exact — *Alopecurus pratensis*.'

The sergeant looked hard at him and slowly decided that the man might be deliberately trying to send him up. Now and again you met them. Dead against the police from the time the nappies came off them — and so many with this mocking politeness — yet bloody villains beneath it all. Well, he knew how to play them — start soft, finish hard. He'd show him. Allopesomething pretences . . . and cheekier — creeping finger grass, saucy sod. He said, 'Oh, well — that's all right, then. Sorry to bother you.'

He walked away, glad he had omitted adding 'sir' to his parting words, and as they moved off said to his driver, 'This world is full of screwballs. Grasses.' He mimicked,

'This one's Creeping Finger Grass — by God, I'll check that at the library and if there ain't no such thing I'll look forward to another meeting with our friend.'

That evening Alfie Grey made a call to Sir John Warboys and gave him a full report on his progress and explained his hopes that what was already becoming a somewhat tedious enterprise might be very soon concluded.

Before he rang off, he asked, 'What's he after, sir — eggs or the young ones?'

'I should think the young ones, Alfie — which means he won't be going after them for at least four or five weeks. Say getting on for the end of May. I should think, if you wanted to, you could come back to London for a while.'

'That's very good of you, sir. But I'd rather not. You see, sir — the wife's gone off to Scotland for a few weeks to her sister so I'd be on me own. And, anyway, sir — he might be popping up for a look at the birds before they're ready to fly. It's an ideal killing ground. I could take him then. And they tell me that in another three weeks the tourist season begins to hot up. Not that I couldn't take him in daylight with people around — but he wouldn't try it then. But any night or early morning he might decide to go and I could get him. Or, you never know, sir, some better chance altogether might come up.'

'You sound as though you like it down there, Alfie.'

'I do, sir. The people's nice, and some of the grasses is quite interesting.'

'All right. Then you stay on.'

★ ★ ★

Three nights later the sergeant who had talked to Alfie Grey at Bossington lay in bed with his wife, awake and breathing heavily against the beer he had taken and an unusually hot night for the Spring of the year, said, 'You awake?'

A mumble from his wife told him that she was and he went on, 'There's some bloody queer things goes on in this world. Democracy and all square and above board is bunk. Not that I didn't know it before and am old enough now not to be surprised by it. But that stinking, cocky little bugger I told you about. Creeping Finger grass — that one. 'Member?'

'Sort of . . .'

'For Christ's sake — do you or do you not?'

'Do.'

184

'Well the Super called me in today. Know what he says?'

'How could I?'

She was coming irritably awake — he could tell by the tone in her voice.

'He says with as straight a face as you like — 'Sergeant, that grass bloke you reported — I want you to know you never saw him or reported him and as far as you're concerned, and me if it comes to that, he doesn't exist unless you come across him with a bloody carving knife in his hand and somebody lying between his legs dead as a steer on a slaughter-house floor'.' He sighed. 'I tell you democracy — feudalocracy's the word or something bloody like it — hasn't even begun to be yet. There's them on top and them below.' He paused for a moment, sighed, and said in a much milder tone, 'Yes he was right about grasses. You know that nice library girl, the one with the big — '

'I know her.'

'Well she looked it up for me and I'll say that for him . . . the little sod wasn't pulling my leg. There really is something called Creeping Finger grass.' He laughed. 'Fancy that. I suppose the order of the Creeping Finger is the highest honour you can get if you're in the Wandering — Ooh!'

He broke off suddenly as his wife kicked

him and said angrily, 'You know I don't like that kind of talk.'

He sighed. 'Okay . . . Okay . . . Funny little bugger, though. My God, there's a lot goes on in this world I'm glad I don't know about. One law for the rich and . . . Ah, well, who cares? The bomb will level us all out in the end . . .'

* * *

On the Friday before the Saturday of the Rugby Club Dance Steve Black went up to Swale Place and Sir Anthony ran through the controls of the car briefly and then sat beside him as they went down the drive and turned up the Exford road towards the moors. He could see — and admire — the gift this youngster had, and which he had marked in so many more of his kind, of falling rapidly into a familiarity with machines. It was with some of them as though they had been born with an extra sense — a mechanical ability and faculty. After ten minutes it was as if he had been driving the car for years.

Sir Anthony said, 'The first time my father let me drive — he had a Rolls-Bentley — I was all of a jelly that I'd do something wrong.' He laughed. 'I realize now that it was because my father was jumping with nerves

186

too — but not for his car, but for me — not wanting me to make a bugger's mess of it. Other people's sons could crash gears and let the steering wander because they hadn't right away got the feel of the car. But not his. You chaps . . . well, its evolutionary now. An inherited characteristic.'

'Dad put me up on a tractor when I was twelve. I ploughed the hundred acres of Black Meadow before I was fourteen. But driving this, well . . . it's like a magic carpet . . . '

They drove up to Exford and over the top to Simonsbath and then out to the coast at Lynton. They stopped on the moor top near Countisbury Hill on their way back and Sir Anthony pulling out his cigarette case and offering it to Steve said, 'I don't use a lot of these nowadays. But just now and again I like one.'

Steve took one of the cigarettes and, as Sir Anthony began to reach out to press the cigarette lighter in the dashboard home, said, 'I don't smoke a lot . . . I keep telling myself I'll give it up. A lot of chaps at the rugger club have . . . Here . . . please, sir.' He held out his hand with his lighter in it, and snapped it into flame. Sir Anthony's hand came back from the dashboard. He bent his head, cigarette in hand and lit it from the flame of the lighter . . . a cheap old lighter he noticed. Nothing fancy about this young man . . . penny plain and straightforward. Never a doubt in his mind probably about himself. Ah, yes . . . he'd worry over the success of a field seeding or the progress of a sickly animal . . . maybe, perhaps, about getting a girl into trouble, but even that would be no great shakes for if a lad and a lassie got led away . . . well, passion's fruiting was usually honoured and legitimized. Lord love us . . . what a pleasant turn up for the book it would have been if he'd had a son to come home one day, half-penitent, half-apprehensive of parental anger, to say that he'd got some high-flown academic, all for women's rights and ban-the-bomb, in the family way.

He said, 'Don't get embarrassed about this . . . but when you get married what will you do?'

They both sat there smoking. Steve was silent and thoughtful for a while, then said, 'Well . . . our place won't hold room for two families, and nothing can be done with it until Dad hands it over to me . . . ' he laughed, ' . . . and that could be a hundred years from now. I suppose, Sir Anthony, that I'll just soldier on. There's a little old cottage down by the stream . . . floods sometimes, but it all could be fixed.'

Sir Anthony said smiling, 'River stay away from my door. Your wife'll like that. Tell you what . . . I've got a small farm that's coming vacant in two years' time. I'd let it go again on a long lease but with an option to buy at some time. I'll speak to my land agents about it and they can send you details. I'd like you to have it. What do you say?'

Steve looked at him frankly, studying the half-smiling face and then noticing for the first time the darkening of the skin under the man's eyes. Everyone knew that he could be a bastard, everyone knew more or less of the trouble between him and his wife and were in strong sympathy with her. Yet here he was . . . hinting, making offers, showing kindness and . . . well, there was no getting away from it, showing him favours and ready to offer more all because . . . well, what? Because he had no son of his own to follow him? He had everything except that — which, of course, made the lack more deeply felt. All work that held men and mankind together was God's work. A man needed strength and faith to weed twenty acres of steep, south-banked strawberry fields by hand. God repaid a man for the care he gave to His land — but, you'd got to give first. That was the deal . . . Damned odd really, sitting here now, smoking the man's cigarettes, in a car such as

189

he could never hope to own for himself unless he came up on the pools, that he felt really close to the man, a closeness that . . . well, how the hell could he put it . . . well, maybe that came from sorrow. There just had to be something really eating away at Sir Anthony to make him come down off his rightful perch and treat him . . . farmer's son Steven Black . . . as though he were in the same class and of the same blood. Somewhere in all this there was something he didn't like . . .

He said politely, 'You've been real kind to me Sir Anthony . . . but I think, if you don't mind, I've got to be getting back. If I'm late for milking time . . . well, my old dad will have some rare words to say . . . '

Sir Anthony laughed, waved a hand for them to move on, and thought, the die was cast a long time ago. The fates had given him in the beginning a love of beauty, the love of God's creation and also of Man's, and then somewhere along the line the love had turned to lust and through lust he had taken the thirty pieces of silver and walked light-heartedly around the corner into the wrong road.

At his side Steve said quietly, 'You're sure about letting me have the car, Sir Anthony? I mean . . . what if some fool backs into me or I get bumped? Some of the lads get a bit careless after they've been — '

'Don't worry. I want you and your party to have it — and to enjoy yourselves. So, cast away all cares.'

★ ★ ★

The following morning Sir Anthony Swale, whose parliamentary constituency was in the North of England, was picked up by a hired helicopter and flown off to a meeting with his constituency agent and various members of the local Conservative Association. Richard Crane saw him off. Before he left Sir Anthony said, 'If any mail comes down for me from London, have a look through it and if there's anything important give me a call.'

With a smile Crane said, 'You mean like some parliamentary or constituency matter?'

'For God's sake, no. That can always wait. You know the rules by now ... open everything except something in a woman's handwriting and faintly scented and anything marked *Private* or *Confidential* even though we both know that very few things are. I shan't be away long. There's little likely to turn up that can't wait.' He grinned suddenly. 'Oh, and give me a ring some time on Sunday. I'd bet on it — but I'd just like to know that the Rolls comes back in one piece from the Rugby Club Dance. And have another think about that Cozens water-colour of the Thames and sailing barges . . . something about it, I don't know. But it doesn't ring true to me.'

Standing away from the down draught Richard Crane watched the helicopter rise and circle and then head away to the north-east. He turned and walked to the great semi-circular rise of steps to the front of the house. As he went up them Lady Swale came out on to the terrace, and stood, head lifted, watching the helicopter grow smaller in the distance. After a moment or two her gaze dropped and met his eyes. Then she smiled and gave a little laugh before she said, 'You can't help being fascinated by him, can you?'

'He provokes other reactions though, at times.'

'Oh, I know that. But that doesn't fuss you over much. You've got a cellar full of treasures. If he died tomorrow you know he will have remembered you more than generously. And you could go anywhere you fancied in time . . . Sotheby's . . . Christie's . . . Parke Bernet . . . or, if you don't want to be in the market . . . well, then, with a little help from friends and in the fullness of time . . . what? Director . . . say of the National Portrait Gallery?'

He smiled, knowing these suddenly rising moods, and the need in her to strike out and hit — not the true offender, but someone like himself who offered affection.

He said, 'I'd rather it were the National Gallery. It pays more. Though I'd settle for the Tate. The money's slightly less. But I prefer a view of the Thames to boring old Nelson and his pigeons. And, anyway, if you feel like this, you know the remedy. Not a long lasting one, but then what salve, what pleasure is?'

She was silent, her breathing taut and short tempo-ed. Then, as she turned away from him, she said, 'If I could do it . . . find a way so that no one would ever know it was me . . . I think I would kill him.'

'I don't think you could. The words come easily enough, but the act needs true desperation. And, if I may say so . . . well, you don't have that.'

'So what remedy do I have?'

'No cure that I know of except something that time will bring only for you to find that your freedom has come too late, perhaps. Meanwhile . . . well, it's a case of gather ye rosebuds while ye may.'

She gave a little laugh. 'So I can, and so I will . . . perhaps even today. You know the truth, of course . . . that although I like you very much there is no more than that — just a language which our bodies speak and in that dialogue near full happiness for me . . . near full except for the shadow of self shame and the undeniable at times agony of emotion when high passion is followed by inexplicable guilt. Yes, guilt there is.' She laughed briefly and went on, 'Odd, isn't it? He treats me like one of his whores and I swear has no sense of guilt or shame. I taking loving comfort from you now and then . . . and for days trail self-condemnation like a weighty great robe, shoulder-bowing and dust-raising, behind me.'

He was silent for a moment or two and then said, 'What is there for me to add? I cheat my employer by comforting his wife. Perhaps that is the essence of all guilt . . . to bring true comfort to oneself or another it is necessary to sin . . . either a little, or perhaps in the grand manner. Do you think he ever guesses or even knows what happens?'

'It has had to cross his mind at least, I should think. That he does nothing is not surprising. What is there for him to do? I am his property . . . with you he knows that I am in good hands.' She gave a dry laugh. 'He likes the role of grand seigneur . . . not only for the rights it brings him but the indulgencies he can grant . . . lending his

Rolls to Stevie Black to take a party to the Rugby dance ... lending me, perhaps because my little sin comforts him for his larger and more numerous ones. All this brings ease to some inner anguish, nameless, but demanding some toll from him. Seven years ago I was still innocent of any other man and stayed so until you came here. Now I have joined the club ... the tit-for-tat club with only one qualification for membership ... to have done unto the other what the other has first done unto you.'

With the hint of surprise, and rising approval in his voice, he said, 'I have not heard you speak like this before ... why now?'

'Because I've suddenly grown up, and realize that what can't be remedied need not be mutely endured, but neither should it be blatantly opposed. From today I become my own woman. And also yours, if you wish, far more fully than ever before yet never lacking discretion. On my part or yours.'

'*Le style, c'est l'homme?*'

'That follows. I like yours. But I should be frank and give you some choice. If he found out ... who could say what he would do? Sack you ... divorce me. Or just shrug his shoulders ... and say, *That's life*. Even pretend, for the sake of his own *amour propre*, not to notice anything.' She laughed suddenly, 'He can — to use his own phrase — be an artful bugger. How much do you need his patronage?'

He shrugged his shoulders. 'I'd get by. But if he knew I don't think he'd rush into anything. Not, anyway, until the sorting and cataloguing has been done. You know, of course, that he's going to leave the bulk of it to the nation.'

'Out of conscience or to offset death duties?'

'Neither, though he hasn't said so yet, but I would say as the *Swale Bequest*, plus a handsome endowment.'

'Pure charity?'

'Well, there was a time when you could buy an indulgence, a rich man's ticket to take one through St Peter's gates.'

She said, with a sudden sharpness, 'I think there are things on his conscience which won't have been very pleasing to St Peter. My role has been that of a silly little woman. A gorgeous handful, as he would say. Made for bed and to grace one end of his baronial table. But I know things about him — and let's face it — so do you. You keep silent for one reason and I do for another — you for your job and me for the status quo. Cowards both. Shameful . . . ' She shrugged her shoulders, reached out and touched the back of his right hand and said, 'So let us compound our shames and make them one this afternoon. Quite frankly . . . I want to be loved with tenderness and then passion, and with no thought . . . only an erotic turmoil of mind and body and of true giving and taking and belonging — ' She broke off and laughed briefly. 'You look embarrassed by my rhetoric. All right, then I'll embarrass you further. There are some things I will not do for him. There is nothing I will not do for you.'

'There lies your revenge, not my pleasure. No, we shall be as the moment and our need for one another make us.'

★　★　★

Sitting in one of the club windows which overlooked St James's Street were Sir John Warboys and a fellow knight of the British Empire, Richard Quint. On the table before them were the second and final pink gins which — on such meetings — were part of their pre-lunch ritual. Apart from themselves there were only two other men in the room, sitting at the far end from them.

Warboys said, 'Why is this place always like a morgue on Saturday mornings?'

Quint smiled. 'Why specify Saturday? It's

197

always like a morgue. Anyway it suits our purpose — if I have guessed correctly the need for meeting you here when I would far rather be at home dealing with the first of the year's bad infestation of greenfly on my roses. Now tell me what has gone wrong, let us decide how to settle it and, having so done, we shall be free to lunch without worry.'

'It is all a matter of pride and professional reputation.'

'I don't care a damn for the first and my professional reputation was always non-existent because we never naturally believed in advertising. However, tell me and I will give you an opinion. Do we have the final choice in this matter — even though we are supposed long ago to have retired?'

'The final choice is ours.'

'About what?'

'Dear Alfie.'

'What has Alfie done?'

'Nothing yet. It is all a question of what Alfie can or cannot do. You see a great element of pride enters into this . . . on the one side that is. And on the other . . . well crudely a saving of expenses, and so on. Alfie you know gets paid on the highest — '

'I know all about Alfie. Let's take that as read. But pride now — there's something I've always thought over-rated because such unpleasant buggers made so much of it. Royal Enclosure at Ascot . . . M.C.C. tie at Lords . . . Brigade of Guards. The men who know all about pride never show it. And that goes for high and low and quick or slow — '

'Or putting a fly over a trout's nose while it's lying under overhanging branches.'

'Or picking off a damned traitor at a hundred and fifty yards with a strong side wind blowing. I get it now. Who wants to stop Alfie from doing that?'

Warboys sighed. 'It's not quite as simple as that. Sir Anthony Swale must be put away. That is his destiny. The teasing question now is — do we let the other people do it or do we carry on and do it ourselves before they can?'

'Oh, that's interesting . . . not that I expected it. They've always had a code of practice for certain types of traitors. Long service, good conduct, and, of course, the purity in professional terms of their image as construed by the similar services of other countries. If Dobbin serves them well between the shafts then the day must come when he is put out to grass to spend the rest of his days in what . . . probably regrets and boredom? But now — this is a turn-up for the book. Well, let 'em do it I say. It saves trouble and a certain amount of ammunition. You don't agree?'

'Partly. But we have to think of Alfie. The last thing he'll be is glad that someone else in some other place and by some other means is going to take over his job. That we'll pay him as though he had done it will be no compensation. And a grumpy Alfie can be a very awkward Alfie when we go to him the next time for some other mission. We'll get a dirty answer. If the matter of pride seems unimportant to you . . . well, just fancy if, as a young lad you'd stalked a rising trout, changed flies three times to tempt him and then when he does take and goes off like a torpedo . . . Dad comes up behind and insists on playing and landing him. What about that?'

'No question about it. Patricide. Anyway I don't see any problem. Both sides are after him, both for their own good reasons. The man is only going to get, one way or the other, what he thoroughly deserves. So — let Alfie stay on the game.'

'Without telling him that the others are after his quarry?'

'Certainly. It wouldn't help him to know. Might do the reverse . . . make him too hasty. No, let it stay as it is. This is one head which must be mounted on our trophy wall. And, my dear Warboys, you underrate Alfie. If they're going to send a man after Sir Anthony

. . . then Alfie will spot him and come to you for instructions if he feels he needs any. As a matter of interest, how are they going to do it?'

'That is not known — but I should doubt very much, my dear Quint, that they've got their own Alfie type. Fifteen years ago, perhaps. but not now. There are dozens of sophisticated ways of killing . . . and frankly I regret them. What private pleasure is there if the coroner, moved by an incomplete autopsy since there is no circumstance to suggest other than natural causes, gives the deceased unimpeded progress to the final rites? No . . . you must give the Alfies of this world, no matter what lingo they speak, the professional satisfaction that — with a worthier and kinder upbringing — would have brought them for their skills honours at Bisley. By the way . . . you should see him with clay pigeons or with a fast bird coming down wind and another following but on a crossing course. Down they come . . . Mind you, he got it all from his father — who was a gamekeeper on one of the Duke of Bedford's estates. Endsleigh, in Devon, I think.

★ ★ ★

Far to the east there was the faintest blush in the sky of dawn as the darkness and shadow began to give way grudgingly to the pale colours of coming day. After taking the others home from the Rugby Dance they had driven down to Bossington and along the rough track out on to the lip of the great stretch of pebble beach. Somewhere beyond the river a curlew called and was answered from far down the ridge.

They walked with his overcoat spread over their shoulders, an arm around each other's waist, laughing now and then at the awkwardness of their gait on the moving shingle, but never losing their hold of one another.

Looking at the not far distant car, she said, 'Why do you think Sir Anthony let you have the car?'

'Dunno, but he did.'

'I think I know.'

'Why then?'

'That nephew of his. He's real touched with religion. Always was, my Dad says. Not much of an heir for a man like Sir Anthony. Bet he wanted someone like you . . . someone more like himself.'

'Me — like Sir Anthony?'

'Don't you think you are?'

'Wish I were . . . with all his money and

that house and . . . though I don't know . . . '
He paused and pursed his lips in thought.

'Don't know what?'

'That I'd want all that responsibility . . . all his pictures and a bliddy great place to keep up even if I had the money.'

'I didn't mean it that way.'

'Then what way?'

'The way you'll promise anything to get what you want — and then when you've got it you'll go straight ahead and break your promise just so long as you think no one will find you out.'

'Here, you giving me a lecture?' His voice was touched with pique.

'Sort of.'

'Why . . . when everything's so nice?'

'Just because of that. Everything is so nice and I want it to stay that way.'

'Come off it, love. You're talking riddle-me-rees. Tell me straight.'

'You shouldn't need any telling about some things.'

'I need telling a lot of things. For instance, how do you know that Sir Anthony is that way or whatever way it is you think he is and that so am I? Christ, I'm getting so mixed up I don't know what we're talking or arguing about.'

'You don't have to swear. And anyway, if

you don't know what I'm talking about then that's a poor look out.'

'Well, that's a lot of help.' He stopped suddenly, and held her by the shoulders, his face full of concern, and then said, 'Hey . . . nothing's gone wrong, has it, because of that time when we . . . ?'

She raised her face to him as they stood in the lee of the car, and said, 'It could be, but I don't know . . . I don't know whether I did it right or . . . I don't know, perhaps I'm just scaring myself. You can imagine what my father will be like — and he'll be after you too.'

'Let him. We're both of age and nobody can stop us getting married. So, come on, cheer up. It's probably all a false alarm and if it isn't . . . well, we'll face it together. Come on.' He opened the door of the car for her and handed her in by the elbow. He went round to the other side of the car and got into the driving seat.

The sun was just clearing the eastern horizon. He started the motor, reached into his pocket for his cigarettes and as he put one in his mouth he stretched out with his free hand to push home the dashboard cigarette lighter. As his fingers touched it he saw her watching him. She shook her head and said, 'No.'

Puzzled, he asked, 'No, what?'

She sighed but there was no irritation in her voice, only the warm tones of love as she said, 'You've got a memory like a sieve. Don't you remember what you said about giving up smoking after the rugger dance? *I'll do it, all right. You'll see.*''

Fingers on the knob of the lighter plunger, he grinned and said, 'Oh, just this one. After all, it will be the last one.'

'All right — have it your own way. I suppose in time I'll get used to not knowing whether you mean a thing or not.'

Fingers caressing the roundel of the plunger, he looked at her and shook his head gently. Women . . . she was probably fussing over nothing, might even know it *was* over nothing but felt that it would be a good thing to give him a fright . . . other chaps had been caught before. Hasty marriage and then no baby. As that thought crossed his mind, he closed his eyes, not wishing to see her eyes on him, nor wishing to hold such a disloyal thought in his mind a moment longer. He turned away, took the cigarette from the corner of his mouth and threw it out of the window as his left hand dropped from the lighter plunger.

Suddenly the absurdity of the situation struck him. There were no certainties in life.

The whole thing could be a false alarm. But baby or no baby — what did it matter? She was the one that mattered. He'd badgered her until she had given in and . . . Christ, what was he? Well, whatever he was, he knew that he was no Sir Anthony Swale. Like him though he might, he was no man to mould oneself on.

He laughed suddenly, throwing back his head and shaking it for a moment or two, then suddenly stopping, his eyes full on her, said, smiling, 'You've been worrying all these days. Keepin' it to yourself. Well, you can give that a stop. If anything happens, I'll do the worrying and the talking and whilst I don't want to put no backs up I'll talk straight. What we've done we've done because 'twas in our nature and our bodies' wanting. Now forget it all — I'm your bloke and anything to be said or done goes through me first. But — ' he grinned suddenly, ' — to give you some comfort . . . aye, and to be a bit frank . . . there's many a time when a wanting cow is put to the bull that nowt comes of it.'

She was silent for a moment or two then with a little cry she moved close to him and put her arms around him. He bent and took her mouth and they stayed in close embrace as the eastern horizon slowly began to flush with the golden-crimson touch of the new day's sun.

Overhead the tiercel, coming back low over the water meadows holding, limp swinging in one claw, the not yet maturely feathered body of a young mallard duck, saw the car and the embracing lovers. He swung away from the sea, went low over the broadening river and then, hugging bracken and gorse, rose towards the long run of the grey point and then slid down the mild pulse of the westerly breeze and found perch not far from the eyrie. His mate dropped down to him and he moved aside with a small cry and half fanned his wings as he faced the rising sun and she began to tear at the still warm breast of the mallard.

* * *

From a call box in Bridgwater, the long esplanade running away to his right and, with the tide full in, and a high wind behind it sending brief curtains of breaking waves sweeping across the road, Alfie spoke to Sir John Warboys.

'Well, as you know, sir . . . he's not down here now. Back in a week, I understand. But if I had a wider briefin' than what I've got . . . well, I could have got him more than once but not to say with certainty. What do you think about that when he comes back, sir?'

'I'll think it over and let you know. In the meantime take your chance if you get a good one — but don't risk anything doubtful.'

'As you say, sir.'

Alfie Grey came out of the telephone booth, looked up at the sky and addressed the scudding bands of grey clouds almost aloud, 'I think I got to go ahead soon and do it . . . even if it's going to be a little risky. Yes, and that . . . ' he chuckled, 'is just about what that old devil Sir John wants to happen. Wouldn't say so — but hopes so. Why not? He may be a gent — but he's got his work to do. Ah, but more than that he likes to make it fun, the old devil. If I could do it in plain daylight and no one to spot me . . . even come up afterwards all moon-faced like, saying . . . 'Ullo then, what's a bin goin' on here? You don't say? Well, rot my turnips and blight me peas, what's the world comin' to? Right through the 'ead, you say? (Have to drop a few aitches and use Cockney or Mummersetshire . . . Not that people remember. They only think they remember.) Fat man kills somebody and runs off and you ask, 'What did he look like?' and they say, 'Oh, I dunno . . . sort of ordinary like.' 'Fat ordinary or thin ordinary? Tall ordinary or short ordinary?' And then some are honest enough to say, 'Well, sort of in between the two like, could be . . . But I didn't get a good look . . . ''

He sighed heavily and then walked to his car and decided that he would go and pay a visit to Mrs Winslade, because it had suddenly struck him that she might be able to help him if he put things obliquely to her. But he would have to be careful . . . Oh, yes. No flies on her.

Still it ought to work. Worth a lot of money, I suppose, if you know the right market? *Don't understand how people can do it. Just because it's rare like some grasses and flowers and too many folk too greedy to give 'em a chance to get less rarefied.* Same with them birds, I suppose . . . And so on till he got a rough time for taking them young hawk things which he'd seen His Highness around too often not to be able to read what might be in his mind. *Sell 'em, can they? Worth a lot of money in the right place, they say. Worth trying.*

She might rumble him but not down to any detail and she'd know from the way he was with grasses that the last thing he would be after would be the young birds. No, she might think all sorts of things, but

never that. Live and let live was his motto
when he wasn't working. And even at work,
why Sir John would never ask him to be
final unless it was to a real wrong-one and
Her Majesty's peace of the realm at peril,
God Bless Her Heart and Long May She
Reign Over Us and not necessarily a quick
death to all her enemies. He smiled
suddenly and went on aloud, 'I'll go the
long way round so I get there just as tea's
being served. Hot toast and cinnamon
— I'll have to tell the wife about that.
Lovely.'

At first Mrs Winslade had been amused
and a little touched by the endearing naïveté
of Alfie Grey. She liked him, of course . . . but
even now, after some growing establishment
of familiarity and mutual trust and near
approach to complete frankness with one
another, she was always aware of a warning
bell ringing distantly whenever he came to see
her or she saw him from afar . . . driving his
car along the coast road or inland towards the
sheep-pocked heights of Exmoor. In her own
mind she could only describe him as being
too good to be true. And more than that
— knowing that he was being too good to be
true but — was she right — wanting to be
like that because underneath the cap and
bells and the twirling walking stick, balloon

festooned, hid a serious, puposeful man, enjoying his own pantomime performance but never forgetting his real role which was . . . and it was here that she ran into a teasing stalemate. What was his real role? Well, today, she felt she knew. Only a guess, of course, but one which, in view of their growing friendship, she felt she could venture to declare in frank terms.

She said, offering him more toast, 'Mr Grey, we've got to know one another quite well. Less than friends, maybe, but more than just acquaintances. Do you think that might give me the right to be a little more frank with you than I have so far been?'

'You be as frank as you like, ma'am. And — ' he gave her a friendly grin, ' — if you come to a point where you just don't know how to say more . . . well, then, I'll help you over the stile. Not that there's a great deal to tell, mind you.'

'Thank you. Of course, you're not just down here on holiday, are you?'

'No. But then partly.'

'You go out to Bossington and Hurlstone Point fairly often, don't you?'

'One of my favourite places when I feel bored.'

'You know about the peregrines out there, don't you?'

'Them birds? Oh, yes.'

She laughed. 'Don't pretend ignorance. You probably know as much about birds as you do about grasses. You see, I think in some way, you're something to do with or working for the Royal Society for the Protection of Birds. And you're keeping an eye on the peregrines out there. Right or wrong?'

'Yes, I'm keeping an eye on things . . . but not officially. More sort of on the side. Some birds, like some grasses, if there ain't many of them around . . . well, they need watching because there's bound to be some unthinking collector itching to get his hands on them. But that ain't what I really do.'

'Then what do you do? Or should I not ask any further?'

Alfie smiled, and said, 'With anyone else, I suppose I would have long ago wriggled out of this talk. But I know I can trust you. What I am really is a sort of . . . well, agent or private investigator . . . or a watcher or a pryer — well there's plenty of names for my kind, and some of 'em far from polite. This is a fast changing world as we both know, and if you want to get on in some walks of life you got to be ready to do it by tripping up the man in front of you and kicking him in the head as you step over him. That's what a lot of people would like to do with your

212

neighbour next door.'

'Sir Anthony Swale?'

'That's right, ma'am.'

'Does he know about it?'

'Oh, no. We never tells that kind of client anything. Makes 'em self-conscious at the best of times and downright jumpy at the worst. This is a wicked world, ma'am. And I have to say that, sometimes, I feel I would like to have found meself a different kind of work. There is this to be said for it, though. I get to travel and have a lot of spare time . . . like now down here because I only cover this end. It's often like that but this time it's different because I've met you, ma'am, and you've been very kind and friendly to me . . . so much so — ' he gave her a warm grin, ' — that I've told you more than I should have done.'

'So you may have, Mr Grey. But I appreciate the compliment and all you've said to me will go no further. I hope you won't mind this — but may I ask, if Sir Anthony knows anything of all this?'

Alfie chuckled. 'You're a one for coming straight to the point. The answer is that I don't know. You see I work for an agency. They know all that sort of thing. I just get me job briefing and that's that. And I must say this — it's only because you're a real

213

understanding lady that I've told you so much. Strictly wrong of me. But sometimes, when you know you're in good hands, it's wise to unload a little of life's problems. Nothing better than a good natter with someone of understanding like your good self, ma'am.' He was silent for a moment or two and breathed deeply twice, sighing somewhat. He'd said more than he had ever meant to and knew that he had done wrong . . . well, professionally. But there it was . . . Funny, he'd never felt like this before. Never sort of stepped back, taken a good look at himself, leave alone almost spill the whole tin of beans to a hardly known, friendly lady whose hair would have stood on end if she could have heard some of his truths . . .

So from Mrs Winslade Alfie learned that if anyone were going to rob the peregrine eyrie it would have to be done before the young birds could fly, which would be soon now, and when, naturally, she asked him why he wanted to know, he said, 'Well, you knows I like it out there in me spare time . . . picked up three or four grasses I wanted for my collection . . . but now and again someone coming along asks me if I know about some peregrines' nest . . . ' He grinned. 'You know, just casual like they are — but although there's collectors and collectors — the decent

214

sort and then the don't-care-a-damn sort — you can never miss 'em if you're one yourself.'

'And what do you tell them?'

Alfie chuckled. 'I says I've never heard of 'em. And I'll tell you — without disrespect — if a chap in clergyman's gear came and asked me I'd do the same.'

An hour later after Mrs Winslade had entertained Alfie to tea he drove down the Dunster road and parked in a small lay-by. Here he pulled out his Pathfinder map of the area — SS 84/94 — 1:25000 — and studied it carefully for a while, whistling gently to himself and feeling happy because something either in the air or his bones, as he put it to himself, told him that he could now pinpoint one likely killing ground . . . in fact, he hoped *the* killing ground. Several times in the past he had seen Sir Anthony Swale walk the shingle ridge to the cliff foot where the peregrines nested. He never put the Rolls-Royce in the car park by the river footbridge, but always drove on down the rough track that led out on to the shingle ridge and left the car there.

From now on Alfie, he told himself, you are — once you know the master's at home — in for some very early rising at Rose Cottage. Yes, he told himself, it was an ideal place. Time — as an eager young officer in his Army days was fond of saying — spent on reconnaissance is seldom wasted. That was a life he couldn't stand. Mistake to try it in the first place. Deserted. Got caught and then one day they hauled him into a room and there was Sir John Warboys . . . and then it all began . . . All because he'd won the Regimental shooting cup, but not really. That and a few other things. He'd said: 'I want you . . . just the way you are. We'll add a few trimmings and you can live the life of old Riley so long as you're not working. What do you like doing most in the world? . . . Collecting grasses, eh? Couldn't be better. Only an innocent man could say that when caught in a field, rope halter in hand and a fine pony grazing. But what do you say about the rope in hand? Nothing? Quite right. Just cut his throat . . . ?' Oh, he was — and still was — a great one for a joke. But bugger me, on a job — watch it. Like now. Cinnamon toast for tea with Mrs Winslade was one thing. Bird fancying with Sir Anthony Swale was another. Still, there was one big comfort — the people he worked for always looked after their own. One law for the rich and another for the poor — but for Sir John's boys no need ever to fear the law. Lovely feeling, too . . .

When he telephoned Sir John that evening and outlined his proposed plan of action he was given full approval for his plan and strict instructions on the movements he was to make after dealing with Sir Anthony Swale. They were the same as they had so often been in the past. The action . . . then the drive away to some designated lay-by . . . there to abandon everything — the machine, his suitcase and any armament — and then, after two more weeks at the cottage, his walk to the nearest bus stop and so to the nearest railway station and so back to London and three weeks or never more than four or five weeks later the machine would be delivered to him in London and his wife would give him an odd look but say nothing. Only once had Alfie ever even obliquely referred to his official affairs. He had said to her, 'Anything ever happens to me — which ain't likely — you'll find I'm well insured. And what I do, I likes doing. Nobody ever pressed me. 'Nuff said? Good.' Aye, protection from the top — the real top — let a man get away with murder. Only he didn't think of it that way. No. For him it was just another way of carrying on his Army service — only now he never wore uniform and, which was pleasing, never had to salute an officer.

★ ★ ★

Sir Anthony came back, unexpected and unannounced, dropping out of the sky in a hired helicopter on the driveway just in front of the house.

His wife, he found, was out. He went down to the underground storerooms and had a few words with Richard Crane, leafed through some of the sheets of the inventory with descriptive notes which Crane was compiling and took pleasure in it. The man had a nice turn of phrase and a lightness of touch which in no way detracted from or devalued his undoubted scholarship.

He said, 'Some time . . . when all this is finished, you ought to settle down and write a book. Not some stuffy old work, but something that would catch the public eye, make you some money and — ' he grinned, ' — get you on T.V. Tell you what you should do — we've got a few examples down here, as you know — write about art forgeries and forgers' mistakes . . . '

'Like the Ioni triptych forgery in the Courtauld Institute?'

'I don't know that one.'

'Pop in and have a look at it sometime. It's a twentieth-century forgery of an early fifteenth-century Annunciation. Then there's that drawing by Augustus John which I think was at the Fitzwilliam Museum, Cambridge.

The Director one day was upset to receive a letter from an artist saying that the work was his and not Mr John's. Apparently the owner of the drawing had asked Augustus to sign a drawing which the painter assumed to be a work of his youth, about which he had forgotten.'

'You never know where you are, do you?' He laughed. Then, his tone changing, he asked, 'Do you know where my wife is? Her car's here.'

'Yes — she's gone over to have tea with Mrs Winslade. Walked over.'

'Oh, and what about the Rolls? Did my young farmer lad bring it back in one piece?'

'Yes. Spotless, too.'

'Well, everything seems to have kept sailing on an even keel while I've been away. Oh, yes — I've just got to go over to Porlock to see someone. You might tell Lady Swale that if she comes back before I do.'

'I will. Before you go . . . ' Crane hesitated for a moment or two, then went on, 'I hope you won't mind my asking. But not once since you've been back — '

Sir Anthony laughed, saying, 'I know what's coming. But I didn't expect you to pick it up so soon. How did you get it?'

Crane smiled. 'Lady Nicotine. Fingers of the right hand. How long's it been, sir?' It was, he thought, the right moment to use a deferential 'sir'.

'The day I left here. And not for any dramatic or medical reason. It just came over me that perhaps for once in my life I ought to use a little of my will power in pursuit of the longterm pleasure of perhaps adding a few more years to my life. Quick of you to spot it.'

'I'm very glad. Funny . . . at first I couldn't think what it was. And then I knew — when you gestured with your right hand. Usually you held your cigarette case in it before taking one, and also you had a habit of going on talking, still holding it. Lady Swale will be pleased.'

Sir Anthony shrugged his shoulders. 'Don't let anyone start celebrating yet. I'm a weak man when it comes to my pleasures. Well, I want to run over to Porlock and get a few things. I shan't be long.'

Half an hour later Sir Anthony parked the Rolls at the end of the rough lane which led from the car park to the shingle ridged beach. Slipping on a cap and raincoat against the sharp squalls of rain which had come with the dying of the afternoon, he slung his field glasses round his neck inside his coat and walked towards the point, keeping just below the leeward side of the pebble ridge. A hundred yards from the foot of the cliff, the sea running shorewards under a rising tide, spume and spray bursting over the foreshore rocks, he found cover behind a growth of sprawling briar growths.

Holding his glasses on the eyrie he could make out no sign of life. That meant nothing, the young if there would have their heads down, huddled together for warmth against the rain bite of the wind. The parent birds would be away hunting. For a moment or two, as the onshore wind slashed a thick veil of rain across the sea and over the beach and the cliffside almost disappeared from sight, he swore to himself and wondered what the hell he was doing here. He owed nobody any favours . . . not even the oil sheik for whom he intended the birds as a gift. Over all that he knew that at heart he was a conservationist. All things of value to mankind should be preserved. That was how he felt about paintings and works of art . . . that was how he felt about his own ancient house and the fields and woods of his estate . . . and, God help him, that was how he had — and still did at times — felt about his wife. But some devil had touched him and passed to him the itch to act and work against all his good sense and good taste . . . to take that which he loved for its beauty and the pleasure that came from cherishing and worshipping its loveliness and, sometimes slowly, sometimes rapidly, corrupt it, pull it apart, degrade it . . . all as though there were some demon in him which awakened without warning and made a mockery of his free will and his deep-seated love of the true, the good, and the beautiful. So much did he feel this, that he wondered how anyone could doubt the existence of the Devil and his evil in this world. And of the truth that the Evil One took more pleasure in the corruption of one true soul than he did in any of the villainies and salacities of his followers . . .

As though — in the midst of his short vigil and deep introspection — some answer was being given him, there came a blaze of lightning from the sea-broken horizon and then a long, low roll of thunder.

A few moments later the tiercel winged up the beach, no more than a man's height from the shingle, passed him a few yards to his left and then rose to meet the upthrust of the headland and settled on the eyrie ledge.

Sir Anthony brought his glasses to his eyes and saw the rise of the two young birds and the mêlée as the tearing and the taking of the prey began. He lay and watched, oblivious of the rain . . .

Later as he walked back to his car he knew that in a week the birds would have to be taken. Beyond that point . . . it would be too late.

He took off his raincoat and tossed it into the back of the car before getting in. Once in, sheltered now from the rain and wind, a momentary nervous shiver of excitement gripped his whole body, binding his body muscles tautly strung against the rise of some deep-seated, ineffable emotion. He smiled to himself at the onset of this rare sensation. Oh, before paintings and sculptures he had known it often . . . the first time he had seen the original Botticelli *Birth of Venus* . . . the first time of making love to some long desired woman . . . the first time fully licensed and full owner of a Porsche he had seen the needle pass the hundred miles an hour mark and the ribbon of road before him being devoured as though the machine were some great beast, ravening and gorging itself on all that lay in its path . . . and his first woman . . . well hardly full woman — one of their housemaids, ever willing to favour him for half-a-crown. But above all his first true ecstasy . . . and bought with his own money and against his father's advice and judgment . . . the day, nervous but determined he had sat in the bidding crowd at Sotheby's and from a sale of English enamels he had bought a *boîte à surprise*, the lid finely painted with an explicit *scène galante* of *Une Courtisane Amoureuse* after Boucher. At this moment it graced his wife's dressing table. Coarse and fine — he could with composure admit — were his two loves and, as far as he could see, that was how it should be. In all things Nature demanded balance. Life and death and the beauty of the falcons opposed to their rapacity, their natural instincts which, surely, were as God given as the aesthetic senses of any connoisseur?

Alfie Grey had seen him come down the drive and turn right towards Dunster and with a little sigh had decided to follow him.

From the moment Sir Anthony had gone straight through Dunster and turned left down the main road to Porlock he had guessed where he was going. The birds must be approaching the taking point. In his last telephone conversation with Sir John Warboys he had been given a brief résumé of the development from egg-laying to birth and on until the moment of first flight of the peregrines. Being a polite man and without presumption, he had not felt it necessary to tell his employer that he had already acquired all this knowledge in one afternoon at the library in Minehead. He knew this following would lead him nowhere, but conscientiousness made him do it. Besides — he thought rather forlornly because he was getting a little bored and tired of this assignment (the ones he mostly had were brief and exciting and always took him back to wife, allotment and pub friends a very refreshed man) — his not to wonder why, his but to do and die. He grinned — not if he bloody well had anything to do with it.

Once or twice, in the beginning, and now more often as he sat at his window overlooking the valley, seeing the long tree-lined drive running up to Swale Place and the movement of occasional cars, people, postmen — Christ, he could give a timetable for a good many of the callers — he wondered why Sir John didn't choose some simpler, quicker way of doing things. For instance, some knife work in a dark alley, and plenty of times and places when a single shot and a fast getaway would have worked without a hitch. Once hc'd had the courage to ask — not Sir John himself — but Sir Richard Quint this question. Sir Richard had smiled, patted him on the shoulder, and said in a fatherly way, 'A very good question. It's all a matter of aesthetic satisfaction. Anyone can shoot a sitting bird. Anyone can blow up a house-full of important people just to be able to kill one particular one of them. Anyone could poison the wine at a dinner party to kill all in order to finish off one. Killing, my dear Alfie, is an art. The first mankind ever practised. No matter what other skills and talents he possesses — deep down he knows and is proud of the fact that he is a killer. Fishing, shooting, hunting, trapping, poisoning . . . all arts, my dear Alfie, and well developed. But the great joy, Alfie, and when man can arrange to have it, then have it he will, is for a while to have the power of life or death over someone while they are unaware of it. That is to be a god. And all men want to be gods. So Alfie — go away and be happy. You are a god and a very special one because you will never know the misery of the Judas kiss. Is all that clear?'

And Alfie remembered that he had said — 'I think it will be when I've thought it all over.'

But it never had been because at some point an instinct had arisen in him which made him suspect that too much thought might take a lot of happiness out of his life. The thing was to be what you were . . . and to do what came naturally. But always be careful even if you had good friends like Sir Richard and Sir John.

Standing now in the narrow beach lane which ran down one side of the car park Alfie had kept his glasses on Sir Anthony as he had moved off and now watched his return to his car, clearly empty-handed.

He walked back to his car and drove off taking a turning which ran down a narrow lane and would eventually lead him to Porlock once he hit the main road. Sir Anthony — not that it mattered much one way or the other, but Alfie liked to stick to the cautionary drills — would almost certainly go back through Aller and out on to the Minehead road. You might think you were being discreet, making no advertisement of your interest — but be around someone too often, although never seen, and the human instinct began to sense an alien occupation with one's activities.

6

Walking slowly from Lancaster Gate, where they had met, Yepikov and Chukolev moved southwards across Kensington Gardens towards the Albert Memorial. Mikhail, wearing a white cap, dark glasses, and a heavy blue serge suit, said, 'How is it to be known for certain that the mechanic man Kirkman did actually fit the appliance? I cannot believe it, since surely it would have happened by now?'

Chukelov waved a dismissing hand. 'It is one of those things. Chance. Twice we have checked the installation. The first time we have a man do it just after Kirkman goes to Holland . . . we have a duplicate key and one of our men goes into the garage while Sir Anthony Swale is away. And then the second time, which is not very long ago, we have send a man down to Somerset and one night he has gone into the garage of Sir Anthony's house and checked. It is all there still, and needs only for the lighter to be used.'

With a faint smile Mikhail said, 'Moscow will think that so far he is a very lucky man.'

'There are such men.'

'And also such unlucky men. It could be

that someone else will use it . . . the chauffeur or someone he lends the car to. You know when I am back in Moscow this time there is a growing feeling that we begin to make the carrying out of simple matters very complicated.'

'Has it not always been so?'

'Maybe. But . . . we walk together because I am here to tell you something which will surprise you.'

'Then it must be something unguessable . . . miraculous.'

'Not so.'

'Then tell.'

'There have been, as you know, a few changes at home, and things are, if not in a muddle, then in a flux . . . what is right one day is wrong the next. It happens for many important things and people yet so far without any great publicity. But it happens too for some not so important people. And so, since the bomb in Sir Anthony's Rolls-Royce has not gone off so far there is now an urgent directive that every step should be taken to dismantle it. Suddenly someone in Moscow — and I could not tell who — has stepped to the side of Sir Anthony and so I bring this new order.'

'But how shall this be done?'

'First — as quickly as possible. It is, of

course, recognized that one could be too late. That is understood in Moscow — but it would be very unpopular all the same and many friendships might be spoiled, if you understand me?'

'Could one not send Sir Anthony a frank message telling him not to use the car?'

'And so inform him that among his good Russian friends there have been those with power who did not like him? Wished him spectacularly dead?'

'I am not deceived. Somewhere, someone has seen a new use to which Sir Anthony could be put. So it is — save him. He is valuable. We need him.'

'Why do you upset yourself? You have followed all orders correctly. Now follow this one. Sir Anthony must be saved, but without ever knowing the danger he has been in. That — Mikhail — is of first importance. Find a man and send him down. You will gain much credit with people of ever rising importance at the Kremlin. Things change . . . a little too often perhaps — but one must be alert to take advantage of all opportunities.'

'And if the worst happens?'

'Do not be pessimistic. I give you a little cheer. From other sources here in London it is said that Sir Anthony is giving up smoking.'

'Is going to or has?'

'How should I know? But keep your fingers crossed.'

Chukolev stopped and lit a cigarette.

Mikhail almost wailed, 'And all this without Sir Anthony knowing or suspecting anything. You ask me the — '

'Ah!' Chukolev stopped him with a raised and admonishing finger. 'Do not use the word. Nothing is impossible. But everything is possible for your future if you successfully protect our friend Sir Anthony and also the honour of our country.'

With a sudden bitterness Mikhail said, 'Sometimes I think you get joy from others' problems.'

'Not so, not so. You found the Maurice Kirkman. You found him. Find another. So that is all arranged. Now I tell you something to cheer you up. These gardens you know are where the Great Exhibition was held in Queen Victoria's reign. You know of the Queen Victoria, of course? A great lady. And related to the Russian royal family. Now, you like that I take you to Fortnum and Masons for tea? That is your favourite, no?'

'No. I shall now have much to do. But thank you.'

★ ★ ★

Five days later, one Adam Foreman — single, forty-five years of age, ex-the Corps of Royal Electrical and Mechanical Engineers, long dishonourably discharged without publicity since at the same time two officers were also involved in the sale of electrical components and equipment and the authorities wished to avoid unfavourable publicity, a cheerful, prematurely balding bean-pole of a man with a stooping gait — was given his briefing as he sat on the edge of one of the fountain basins in Trafalgar Square, with pigeons strutting round his feet.

Foreman listened attentively to his briefing, nodding now and then without speaking, and then said, 'What about the money?'

'Half now and the rest when you've done it.'

'Three-quarters now and the rest when it's done. If not — don't say any more.' He made to rise and go.

A hand gently held his arm and restrained him.

'Agreed. Now listen — you want it on paper or can you carry it in your head?'

'Don't worry. Nothing to it. Just give me the general form. Dismantling a job is always twice as easy and twice as quick as setting it up. Oh, and another thing — what about dogs?'

'Small terrier, sleeps in the house, and a couple of gun dogs which are kennelled behind the keeper's cottage a quarter of a mile away. You do understand that this is something we wish to be done urgently?'

'I'll make it as quick as I can. Say a week at the most. Got to look a place over first, you know. Got to think of my own safety. But don't you worry.'

Two days later Adam Foreman (who had booked into a Minehead Hotel late the previous day under a false name) motored up the Dunster-Timberscombe road along the Avill brook and got his first look at Swale Place but, owing to the curve of the drive after it crossed the stream, he could see little of the house and nothing of the stable and garage yard. From his map he saw that he could go farther up the road towards Timberscombe, take a turning to the right and reach a higher road that ran back parallel to the valley road below and that along it somewhere he should be able to get a much better view of Swale Place.

Thirty minutes later he drew up on the open piece of ground adjacent to Rose Cottage. Sitting in the car he took up his binoculars and focused them on Swale Place. The view was perfect with all he needed laid out before him as though he were looking at some small-scale model of a country house in an exhibition ... the curling line of the brook, the drive gates and the bridge over the stream, the gate-keeper's house to the right — there was a man in shirt sleeves trimming one of the hedges with shears — and then to the right of the big house itself the large stable yard and — as though laid on for his especial benefit — one of the old stable buildings had its doors wide open and just outside a man was hosing down a small car — looked like a Renault, he thought — while in the building itself quite plain to see, facing him, was the Rolls-Royce. As a bonus he could see there was a footpath from the bridge that followed the near hedge of an adjoining meadow all the way up to the west side of the garage yard.

A piece of cake, he told himself. Do it the first cloudy night. Whole thing a lot of bother, though. Surely all they had to do, whoever they were, was to give the chap an anonymous ring on the telephone. Unless of course — he could see this — they didn't want him ever to know that he'd been marked and now for some reason was being unmarked. He sat, glasses to his eyes, taking it all in and half-whistling a little waltz tune to himself. Park his car up the road a bit, go back and over the drive bridge, then cut away to the right and walk up behind the hedge of the field until he was on a level with the yard ... yes, no trouble. But don't take no chances, not with going or coming back, or with that bloody arrangement underneath. Still they'd given him the blueprint of that ... no need for jacking up to take it off, not like fixing it on all neat and tidy ... just reach your hand in, feel for the wires and get the cutter on them. No need to be tidy. Anyone finding the odds of wires later ... well, that would be a nice little mystery. Life's full of them.

Alfie was having his afternoon rest, and on most days he needed one since he had to be an early morning riser in order to keep an eye out for Sir Anthony. If any of his cars started down the drive then he had to be after the noble baronet even if he didn't end up on the beach which once or twice he hadn't — going right-handed, when he hit the main road, towards Taunton and Alfie following until it was too far into the new day for Sir Anthony to do a smart about turn and head for the beach. In the evening it was the same thing — though less probability of Sir Anthony making a move. From late afternoon until dusk he watched the house and driveway from his bedroom window.

Today when he woke from his afternoon

kip and went to the window to see what the weather was doing he saw Adam Foreman standing by his car on the hillside green watching Swale Place through binoculars.

Alfie at once stepped back from the window far enough to be unseen but able to see. The car driver could be an ordinary sightseer — certainly the view was lovely enough to hold most people . . . but on the other hand Alfie fancied there was something about his stance and obvious interest which might mean he had more than a casual tourist's curiosity in Swale Place. Anyway — you never knew. He memorized the car's make and registration number and noticed that the man was not interested in looking at any other part of the far valley side than the Swale estate. As for the man . . . well, one thing was certain. He was somewhere about the same class as himself. No gent — but no slop either. The car was oldish but in good condition and well kept. He watched him for ten minutes and in all that time the glasses were mostly on Swale Place and its grounds. When the man finally got back into his car and drove off Alfie was charitable enough to give him the doubt . . . some tourist nosey-parkering — but life was full of upsets. He could be something else, so he reported him to Sir John Warboys that evening and gave him the car make and number. The following evening Sir John told him that the man was one Adam Foreman, a motor engineer, clear of any criminal record except — many years back — a dismissal from the Army for dishonestly acquiring War Office property and selling it to a small ring of black marketeers. The kind of thing, said Sir John lightly, that very often happened with the best of quarter-master sergeants. Not to worry. And the first chance you get — we'd like to hear that you have disposed of Sir Anthony. But take no big risks. By which Alfie knew he meant being caught on the job with the rifle hot in his hands and the deceased's eyes fluttering in the last of death's agonies a hundred yards away. Not even Sir John could play Miracle Man on his behalf. Nor, thought Alfie, would he have to so far as he was concerned. A man in the last resort had to look after himself. If you can't do the job, don't take it. If you take it ... well, the best insurance was common-sense and caution and patience. Aye, patience. No rush. Wait until the stars were right and your horoscope read — *Shortly a long-wished-for event will bring you happiness, though sadly at the expense of another who, however, will be neither relation nor friend.*

Frustration sat on Adam Foreman's shoulders like the old man of the sea. The night of his first visit to Swale Place, the garage doors were shut but not locked — though had they been locked he could have dealt with that. When he slipped inside — small tool kit in his hand — it was to find that the Rolls-Royce was not there. Though he was not to know it — Alfie Grey could have told him where the car was, since he had learnt it from Mrs Winslade when she had called and taken tea with him at his cottage and the day being fine they had taken it on the front veranda . . . or, more accurately, large porch, but nevertheless a sun trap with a magnificent view. They had seen the car come down the drive and Alfie, unreasonably but mildly concerned had said, 'Wonder where his Lordship is off to?' And she had obligingly told him that Sir Anthony was going to Taunton for a Masonic dinner and was staying the night there. She knew because she, herself, was going to have dinner with his wife that evening.

It was that night that Sir Anthony permitted himself to break his non-smoking vow — to the extent of allowing himself a couple of cigars during the evening. The second night Foreman was frustrated again.

Sir Anthony and his wife drove to Barnstaple to take dinner with friends and when they returned Sir Anthony ran the car up to the steps of the long front terrace of the house, locked and left it there for the night, and omitted to switch off the single terrace light which meant that Foreman would have had to work — even if only for twenty minutes — in full view of the front windows of the house. Tempted though he was, he decided that the risk was too great to take. As he went back to his car across the fields there was an edge of angry impatience in him. He could have taken the risk. Fifteen minutes' work and everyone sound asleep, but — and that was it. This was one of those *but* jobs — but nothing was to be risked to make it go wrong, to invite some simple act of fate, coincidence, jinx or the sly nature of Lady Fortune — provoking her to stick her meddling finger into the affairs of honest working men . . .

* * *

Richard Crane, lying in bed in the dark, had heard the car come back, watched the brief wheeling of its headlights across the window and held clearly in his mind a picture of her at Sir Anthony's side, fur cape drawn up close about her neck, arms crossed and her hands clasping her evening bag. He had told Sir Anthony that day that he was leaving at the end of the month . . . Oh, yes — he could recommend someone to take his place . . . and, anyway, the bulk of the work was done.

Once he had made the decision and told Sir Anthony of his intention he had felt the edginess of a deep frustration begin to pass away. She had yet to be told . . . unless perhaps, Sir Anthony had already told her. Either way it made no difference because he knew that she had long ago — and their relationship had not altered this in any way — resigned herself to the emotional drudgery of being Sir Anthony's creature. He did what he wished with her and she had neither defiance nor defence . . . she was plastic . . . a woman long ago conditioned and moulded in a way, ironically, that Sir Anthony had never intended.

Now and again with him she had shown spirit and unexpected passion . . . yet both, he knew, arose from despair and a sense of lost self-respect. And poor Sir Anthony, since poor he was even though he had the means to buy paintings and sculptures that all people of aesthetic sense envied him . . . yes, poor, because, despite all the other women, he had chosen unwisely, deceived by a flaw in the strongest of his senses . . . the erotic. He regarded God as the Great Artist and Women His finest work and all of them, like sculptures and paintings, able to be purchased if you had the money. Yet, poor man, he could not bring one genuine tear to his wife's eyes, nor by his touch and caress raise her pulse rate and feel the slow, all possessing deep love-shudder take her and bring the long moan of surrender to her lips.

He laughed quietly to himself and then said almost aloud, 'But, by God, there's no man with a truer eye or touch. And I'm sorry for him because nothing can stop him looking for the thing he can never have . . .'

★ ★ ★

Although she liked him, Mrs Winslade was now more than ever convinced that there was something wrong about Alfie Grey. At times, in talking to her, he seemed almost to invite suspicion — because perhaps deep down he enjoyed the thought of the confusion and puzzlement he gently but persistently created. He seemed to be inviting doubt and the mild suggestion of mystery . . . of an alter ego — perhaps his true one — which he had left behind somewhere while he enjoyed the liberty of playing a role which, given the chance, he would like to have been able to claim as his solely. His real life was a charade. He only came alive when he was set free to play a character part . . . perhaps always the same character part — but even so, certainly a part satisfyingly distanced and different from his real self.

In a way, she supposed, most people found for themselves another self. It was a natural mode of compensation for what they really were. Nobody could be perfect, nobody could from the early years shape and discipline themselves into a chosen and praiseworthy mould . . . but most tried, and some persuaded themselves that they had succeeded. But the honest ones gave up and accepted what they were — imperfect, unreliable, governed by small greeds mostly and larger passions occasionally, promising themselves each morning to do better and going to bed dissatisfied and suing for forgiveness and promising to do better next time. It had come to her slowly that Alfie had another self. With the passing of time and the slow growth of their acquaintance she had begun to feel that he even wanted her to know it and would welcome the relief of being able to talk about it to someone of understanding. So much so had she felt this that — when she had taken tea with him at his cottage one day, the table in the little bay window commanding a view across the valley to her home and Swale Place — she had found herself saying, 'Mr Grey, I like you very much, and I hope you feel that way towards me.'

'I certainly do, ma'am.'

'Good. Then I hope you will forgive me if I say something very personal. And I shall understand, of course, if you prefer not to answer anything positively.'

'I don't know what you've got in mind, ma'am — but I can tell you I'd never be less than polite and also as frank as I can possibly be.'

'Then tell me — if you can — why are you so interested in Swale Place and Sir Anthony and Lady Swale?'

Alfie gave a little chuckle. If you stayed long enough on a job someone always got to notice or to suspect or even just to feel the edge of some uneasiness. It was unavoidable and usually, as now, meant you'd been too long on the job (unavoidable often, but still unsettling). He knew full well that he'd been too long on this one and — given sole initiative — would have finished it long ago. Only Sir John Warboys had worked out the way he wanted it to be. As far from the political as it could be. Conservation, the

Royal Society for the Protection of Birds, Greenpeace . . . Passions rose high these days over the slow stain and corruption of the world's green peace and the raping of Nature's bounties. A week ago Sir John on the telephone after he had made his report had said, 'I'm sure he's going to take the birds . . . a present, a welcome *quid pro quo* for some gift or favour. Play the bird lover fanatic, Alfie . . . take him red-handed . . . save the birds . . . *Let the wild falcon soar her swing* . . . let Greenpeace reign. The gods are on your side. What better killing ground, what sounder motive for a fanatical, unbalanced killing? The world is full of cranks — be wise and join their ranks.'

'I could have to wait a long time.'

'No. Before this fortnight's out they will be airborne. Then before the young birds begin their peregrination send Sir Anthony on his. And don't worry about yourself. Democracy and ineffable justice are only for ordinary mortals. Rarer minds flourish only in carefully regulated conditions. True justice, sadly, can only sometimes be achieved by the abasement of truth and the denial of someone's human rights. Always has it been so.'

Now, to Mrs Winslade's question, Alfie replied without hesitation since hesitation, he

244

had long ago learnt, left a gap through which disbelief could slip to mar the smooth passage of gentle lies. He said, 'Since you ask and I'm an honest man and anyway shan't be giving anything away that you don't know, or perhaps have guessed, and certainly something of which you will approve . . . Well, certain people have employed me to keep an eye on them peregrines until they are full flighted. And these same people, who shall be nameless, think Sir Anthony might try to take one or both to make a present of to one of his Saudi Arabian friends and business chums. I've had all the dope about when it's likely to happen and I can tell you that as from tomorrow morning I shall be up before first light and watching his driveway.'

'But how can you stop him?'

'By being there. He's not going to risk his reputation. From up here long before first light I can see his headlights coming down the driveway . . . so you see, that's why I likes to get a longish kip in during the day sometime.'

Mrs Winslade was silent for a moment or two and then looking Alfie full in the eyes asked, 'Is this the full truth?'

'Why not? There's people with money these days who're mad about conservation — save the whale, save this, save that . . . they'll pour

245

money and time into it. And it's right there should be — though I think there are other causes, less dramatic, less appealing, which far more deserve help. So there you are, that's me, ma'am. Until them birds have flown the nest I've got to keep an eye on them the best I can. I done it before, you know — ' he succumbed, to the pure pleasure of developing a lie artistically, fleshing out the bare bones of deceit into the fullness of received truth and the almost self-intoxication of believing every word of the lies he was uttering . . . such is dedication, he told himself, 'Yes, I've done it before . . . with badgers, young seals, and the protests like battery hens and forced feeding for turkeys and then all those veal calves . . . horrible some of the things I've seen.'

And Mrs Winslade believed him. Why should she not? What possible other reason could there be for his conduct? A common, though likeable little man, but without doubt a true lover of nature and fanatic about grasses. And more than that — in those sturdy, square, battered-looking hands of his there was a delicacy of touch and control she could never have expected until this afternoon she had seen lying loose on a side table before they took tea two or three sheets of drawings on which in pencil he had sketched a small group of primrose blooms . . . and a flowering stem of yellow Star of Bethlehem . . . '*Gagea lutea*,' he had said. 'I found a little patch on 'em up in the woods.' And to her surprise she had heard him hum lightly to himself — 'Star of beauty, star of light . . . ' Extraordinary man!

Before leaving she had said to him, 'Going back to our early conversation, Mr Grey . . . if it should come to a confrontation with Sir Anthony I advise you to handle him very carefully. I'm sure that provoked he could become very violent.'

'Not to worry, ma'am. I knows how to look after meself.'

★ ★ ★

Lying in bed awake she heard the clock over the garage in the stable block begin to strike four. As its last note died away a little owl called from the hillside behind the house and then, from the adjacent room, came first the sound of her husband coughing and then of his movement across the room. The noises that followed were of his dressing, the *clump* of shoes, the opening and shutting of drawers and wardrobe with no attempt made to mute the sound of his movements, and gave her no curiosity. He was a bad sleeper and often rose from bed long before morning to walk the estate or sit downstairs, reading, and more often to go down to the cellar galleries to work or sometimes — as he had in the early days told her — just to sit and look at a picture or a piece of sculpture.

A phrase of his from those early undisturbed days came back to her. 'Looking at a painting or a piece of sculpture is not just looking. That's the thing most people do in art galleries. What, on average little more than a minute at the most to a picture? No. You have to sit and look and go on looking until you've forgotten you're looking and have become part of the picture or piece . . . gone right into it and through it to the artist beyond . . . to the men and women who once faced the blank canvas or the unshaped block of marble and saw in their mind's eye the life and beauty waiting to escape, crying for release . . . ' Although she had done this she had had to admit to herself that it made no difference. The thing she carried always in her mind — perhaps it was of people as well, and so she had married him — was the first impression. The sharp catching of breath when she had walked into the Prado and seen her first Goya. The first time she had seen him . . . that memory long dulled but still coming palely to recall. How different now.

How mistaken she had been. And weak. She could have stood up to him or she could have walked out on him, but instead she had hung on because she lacked the spirit to rebel openly . . . to walk away. 'There will always be ups and downs, my dear,' her mother had said. 'But the wise thing to do is to face things as they come. Everything will fall into place in time.'

She heard the door of his dressing room close and his footsteps as he passed her room. She had no curiosity about his movements. Time was an element which little troubled him. Routine might shape ordinary people's lives, but he lived by his own impulses, though, when he needed, he could be as conventional as the most hide-bound conformist. She turned over and sought sleep . . .

★ ★ ★

Adam Foreman had driven up the valley just before midnight and parked his car in a small lay-by about a quarter of a mile beyond the drive entrance to Swale Place. He sat for a while listening to the radio and then, setting his small alarm clock, made himself comfortable in the back of the car under a couple of blankets and went to sleep. Four o'clock was the hour . . . the soundest part of the night when even the uneasy in mind or body drifted away into limbo or all-solacing oblivion. See this job done tonight and get out of it, he said to himself. The country bored him. He longed for London and its endless diversions. Well, just fifteen minutes alone in the garage and he would be free. He fell asleep quickly as do all men who are untroubled by self-doubt or plaguing imagination that shapes a variety of immediate futures all deformed at some point with the unnatural growth of possible disaster or failure. Fifteen minutes he needed and the job was simple . . . and after that, away with a smile on his lips and money to come for a job well done. And no doubt about being fully paid to make up what had already been advanced. In ordinary business sharp practice was normal. But in this kind of affair trust and loyalty were top priorities. Where everyone has something to lose there was no room for sharp practice. Taking a sucker for a ride was one thing. Playing silly buggers or over clever with a professional was asking for a sharp reaction unadorned with words. A night bird called unexpectedly from the gloom of the woods above the lay-by. To an ornithologist the sound would have been marvellously unexpected and an event not to be commonly disclosed to every Tom, Dick and Harry. It was the soft *koo-eek* of a nightjar, a dying breed. Foreman lay back, worked his body into a comfortable position and fell almost at once into a light cat-nap.

Two hours later, not far away on the hillside above the valley road, Alfie Grey switched off the alarm which had wakened him, rose and dressed without the benefit of washing or shaving. The night and his vigil allowed no time for such refinements. When he returned with the day at full light there would be time and more for such civilized habits. Sometimes he wondered, because he liked toying with such tricks of the unorthodox and word-mixing, whether cleanliness being next to godliness wasn't all nonsense. Surely the holy hermit in his cell or cave had never bothered with it much? And Adam and Eve . . . had she been a stickler for hygiene? Cleanliness was next to godliness. Was it? Now take St Francis of Assisi . . . which he did, whistling gently to himself in the dark . . . and then found himself thinking as he finally sat down at the window to watch the far drive of Swale Place that it must be now any morning because there could be no doubt that within the week the young falcons would be flying and then there could be no hope of Sir Anthony Swale taking them . . . and then, what would happen? God knew.

Perhaps Sir John Warboys knew. All he knew was whatever was wanted to be done could be taken over by someone else. This job had been too long already and he wanted home and his wife and an end to present play-acting. Enough was enough.

★ ★ ★

He came across the field path from the road, the way familiar to him now, and into the stable yard at its top, over a small stile. The night was dark, overcast, no stars or moon, but his eyes were adjusted to the gloom. Morning and sunrise were two hours away. Up the valley a dog barked . . . at least, he called it dog to himself, but it was a fox vixen soon to cub. If the garage doors were locked he would jemmy them open. Once the job was done it didn't matter a damn what people might do in the way of guessing. Doors broken open and nothing taken. He smiled to himself. The mystery of the century.

The doors were unlocked. He turned the wrought iron ring and raised the catch, opening the door just enough for him to slide in and then close it behind him. He stood for a moment letting his eyes adjust to the deeper darkness in here. Then, anxious to get this simple job done, he went round the car to the left hand side of the long bonnet, stood for a moment taking from his pocket spanner and pliers and letting float through his mind the long-studied blueprint of the explosive fitting. All he wanted was to disconnect the firing mechanism from the explosive slab and take both away. All the wiring he could leave without caring a damn. Big mystery some day . . . but who would care? Why worry about the future?

He was about to switch on his torch when from the yard outside he heard a man cough and then the steady sound of footsteps coming towards the garage.

There was nothing wrong with his reflexes. Parked under the window was a smaller car. He moved to it quickly and slipped between it and the wall. He kneeled down, shielded from sight and waited. The footsteps stopped at the main doors and, as the man coughed again, the left-hand door was swung back against the outer wall of the garage. A few moments later and the right-hand door was also opened. A man came into the garage and went to the Rolls-Royce. With a sudden dismay Foreman knew that this was not his night. No disaster hung over his head, only frustration . . . he was going to have all to do again. Another night, maybe nights, in a lay-by . . . he bit his lower lip with frustration.

The sidelights of the Rolls came on and then the headlights. The motor was started . . . ran sweetly and then the car was backed out of the garage. From his hiding place Foreman saw the lights of the car pick up the buildings of the yard and, without knowing he did so, he swore loudly and profanely as the Rolls slid away across the yard.

Five minutes later, tool kit in hand, he was making his way back across the fields towards his parked car.

Alfie Grey saw the Rolls-Royce. He had slept badly and dreamt a lot . . . and it had been one of those nights when his dreams gave him no pleasure. There was no wandering delighted in some Eden where all the grasses which grew were unknown to him so that his specimen book was soon full and there was the promise ahead of hours of pleasure identifying them. He was up at least half an hour before his usual time and just as he finished dressing he saw the car coming down the driveway in the valley with its headlights dipped. He watched it turn out on to the Dunster road and move away.

Well, Alfie — he asked himself — surely this has got to be it? A man could wait too long and then all the pleasure began to run out of a job. Well, good for Sir Anthony. He had moved just at the right moment to keep him in a good humour.

Sir Anthony would drive now down to the beach beyond Bossington. He would sit there out on the brow of the pebble ridged beach at the end of the rough track that ran by the car park. And — Alfie smiled to himself for this had occurred to him in the early days — he would choose a night of dropping tide. Without doubt he had worked out the timings from the tables. When the palest of pale indications came that dawn was on its way then that would be the moment when the headland cliff foot would be free of the sea, and that would be the moment when, having walked there from his car in semi-darkness, Sir Anthony — sack strapped to his belt — would begin his climb. He would waste no time. In little more than fifteen minutes from then he would be back at his car with the young birds and driving away. And if luck were going to run with him, he might have gambled that no one would notice the birds had gone for a few days . . . or, if they did, might even think they had already flighted.

So Alfie made himself a cup of coffee, ate a chocolate biscuit with it, and then carrying his gun case went out to his car. It was still dark and there was the occasional drift of a light shower. He drove slowly, seeing in his mind's eye all that was to come. Hearing, too,

the voice of Sir John Warboys . . . *He'll almost
certainly do it just before first light, and you'll
want all the light you can — so let him go up
and get the birds. Then take him on his way
back. That means a closing range in a better
light. All to your advantage — even you,
Alfie, aren't infallible, but you're as near to it
as makes no difference. Just take him when
he comes back. And what about the birds you
say? Just put 'em back on the cliff foot — the
old birds will deal with them.*

It was at this point — and not for the first
time in his employment with Sir John
Warboys — that Alfie had said, 'Why do you
always — if you'll pardon the liberty, sir
— have to fancy it up like this? I could take
him any day, at any time with two hundred
yards between us and without need to worry
meself over much about meself?'

'I know you could, my dear Alfie, but
— and I hope you will understand this — it is
a matter of charity which is not to be
withheld I hold from the worst of men when
they are killed in the interests of the public
weal. The murderer used always to be allowed
a choice of his last supper . . . tripe and
onions with a bottle of Bass . . . or steak
Diane and half a bottle of Mâcon or
whatever.

'One always owes a last favour to the worst

of men. I assure you that if Sir Anthony were given the choice between this way and, say, a stab in the back in a dark side street he would choose this way. Undoubtedly. So we are merely being courteous without his knowledge. And the comprehension of courtesy, Alfie, no matter how many people would differ, is one of the essential differences between men and beasts.'

Just over half an hour later Alfie switched off his lights as he covered the last hundred yards through Bossington and turned into the small, hedge-sheltered car park. It was a clear starlit night. As calmly as though he were going out to meet the first dimity light to bag a few rabbits, he took the .404 magazine rifle from his car, slung it over his shoulder and walked across the narrow river bridge. It was still dark, but the sky was star bright. His eyes soon adjusted to the darkness and he walked without hurry down the riverside until he came to the point where the wood ended and the path turned sharply uphill to the right on to the cliff walk to Hurlstone Point. He climbed over the gate of a field which, bordered on one side by the tree-lined river, ran away to the high shingle ridge above the beach. He walked a little way down the river until the trees ended and then stopped. Beyond the river and obliquely to his left he could see the dark bulk of the Rolls-Royce. Alfie sat down on an old ant hill, put the rifle behind him so that no touch of star shine should take it, hugged his arms around his knees and waited. Waiting was no hardship to him, since, when he waited like this, there began to creep over him the flesh-raising gentle pleasure of anticipating the near future. There was no fun in this job . . . he thought . . . unless you made it for yourself. Unless you were all eyes and ears and finely controlled muscles. It was on him now . . . the feeling . . . like going back, being the first man somewhere, walking dry-throated . . . knowing something was going to happen . . . and knowing that he could deal with it . . . Oh, he could deal with this all right and be blessed glad to have it done. Not that some of the time and some of the company hadn't been good. It was nice being away from the wife . . . but there was a limit to that. It was nice making friends with Mrs Winslade . . . Funny, he'd only heard recently that her old man had chucked himself off the cliff up there. Nobody seemed to remember why. He'd have thought that anyone married to Mrs Winslade could have counted himself lucky . . .

A moth blundered into his face and he brushed it away. Nasty things. He gave a little shudder. Yes, a nice lady — but no flies on her. Donkeys years ago, though. People change. Or do they? Underneath they go on being the same. You take Sir John Warboys. Real toff and God knows what devilry he hadn't set up in his time . . . Oh, all in the name of Her Majesty's Government — but that didn't make it right, sprinkle it with all the holy water in the world and it wouldn't sparkle with purity. Look at this now — poor bloody Sir Anthony Swale. All right . . . for some reason he'd got across the Government boys — and here he was to do the poor bastard . . . but no trial. Not open. So you could hear or read all. No. And in the end a lot of the . . . well, bad parts of it . . . came down to the likes of himself. Oh, there were others. He knew that. 'Course there was, and God forgive him, no end of a kick in doing it. In knowing the moment was coming. In the moment and right after. Not that he was much of a one for women, well not at all hardly. But he'd had one once — unbelievable! — and that was like this other — like when you did it you felt you were swinging right up there to the stars 'cos that was your proper place. Had to be, otherwise you wouldn't do it. Look forward to it. No hope ever of being different. It was a fix for all fixes. So be happy.

A fish jumped in the nearby river, some buzzing bug went singing past his head, and back in the woods an owl hooted three times. Just, he thought, as though it had been a signal because from beyond the river he heard the sound of a car door closing and a few moments later he saw the dark silhouette of a man walking along the crest of the pebble ridge in the direction of the cliff point.

He made no move until the man moved off the pebble crest to his left and dropped out of sight. Alfie then stood up and walked down the river bank to the bottom of the field where the river took a sharp turn to the right. In the darkness Alfie waded carefully across the shallow run of water. He had picked the spot in daylight days before. On the other side of the river he went carefully up the bank until he reached the pebble ridge. He went right-handed along the bottom of its slope for fifty yards, crouching as he went, and then on knees and elbows worked his way up the few yards of the ridge until he was at its crest and had the whole run of the beach and the sea and Hurlstone Point before him.

He snugged himself down, his body sloped at a slight angle which brought the run of shingle bank and beach into his sight. Backing the prospect was the dark-shadowed, amorphous loom of the high point blocking the end of the beach and rising high against the star-lit night sky, a sky now just beginning to be touched by the faint loom of the nearing dawn. Five minutes, Alfie told himself, and the light would be enough for him since the distance was not far and there was a star reflection from the sea. No more than a hundred yards. One shot. A quick check to make sure that he could honestly claim his paying off money and then away with the birds to climb a few feet up the cliff flank and leave them for their parents to deal with . . . not even Sir John could ask more from him. Anyway, Sir John didn't really care a damn about the birds. Top priority was Sir Anthony . . .

Somewhere in the gloom along the surf line came the high shrill whistling of a flock of birds passing, and high overhead the rising drone of a transatlantic jet coming in. Alfie, rifle covering the stretch of beach, worked his body and elbows down into a comfortable, solid firing position and out of habit licked a forefinger and reached out and touched the foresight.

The little flock of plaintively crying birds came back along the tide line and Alfie said to himself, 'Come on — Come on.' A little more light wouldn't come amiss but not too much . . . he wanted to be away from the car park while it was still a more or less sleeping world.

Then, away ahead of him, he suddenly heard the crunch of feet on the loose pebbles. He breathed deeply and waited and then saw out of the shadowed far foreground the movement of a shape which resolved itself slowly into the form and gait of a walking man.

Alfie covered the moving shade and let the foresight ease slowly to the left with its movement. Instinct more than any conscious calculation had already signalled in him the conjunctions of time, movement and place for the final slow contraction of forefinger, the moment of essential stillness and negation of his body, breath held and no thought in mind, no blood, heart or humanity in his whole being . . . just an Alfie machine, finely programmed, and waiting the dropping of the switch to bring it into action.

He fired and saw the man fall. Although the shot and its echoes were damped a little by the noise of the beach breakers, there was a momentary burst of sea-bird cries as a foraging flock of dunlin on late Spring passage rose in a swift wheeling cloud and winged away down the beach. The sprawled shape high up on the beach lay still.

Alfie stood up and began to walk towards

the dark patch, something without recogniz-
able form until he came closer and saw that
Sir Anthony lay flat on his face with his arms
stretched out in almost cruciform shape, his
left hand holding a wide spread small sack,
his right arm awkwardly doubled under him.

Alfie walked around him. He was in no
hurry now. Blood masked part of the man's
left cheek, blood without colour, dark in the
feeble light. One hand still held the sack. For
a moment or two Alfie was tempted to leave
things as they were, but the thought was
almost instantly rejected. Sir John had never
short-changed him and it was no part of his
nature now to fall prey to such a temptation.
Honest Alfie. He had to put the birds back.

He bent down to take the sack from the
man's hand and, before he could touch it, its
neck still clasped in Sir Anthony's hand, its
shape and size and the way it lay on the
pebbles told him that it had to be empty. It
was almost the last conscious thought that
Alfie had for, at that moment, Sir Anthony's
right leg swung viciously sideways, caught
Alfie's feet at the heels and brought him
sprawling to the ground, his rifle clattering
away from him over the pebbles. Instinct and
training prompted every body muscle he had
to turn the fall into a vicious roll, hands
seeking the other's throat as he went. But

even as his fingers found Sir Anthony's face and began to drop desperately downwards to take his neck the man rolled with him and lay over him and his right hand came down, holding a smooth beach stone . . . no pebble . . . but a killing stone the size of a cricket ball. The stone was smashed into Alfie's forehead, and smashed again and again into face and forehead until the survival frenzy died in Sir Anthony and he rolled away from the still body. The bloody and stone-smashed face of Alfie lay tilted towards the first orange and red touch in the sky of the new day and overhead, flying as though in black choir and sounding an irreverent requiem, went a trio of jackdaws awake from their cliff roosts to the new day's promise of the plundering of eggs and defenceless nestlings along the great curve of the bay.

Above the beach, high on Hurlstone Point where for the first night ever they had roosted away from their nesting site the falcon and the peregrine and the two eyases — first and clumsily flighted the previous evening — watched the growing dawn signal its coming. Before the day was out their first clumsy flight would be transformed and they would move with ever-growing confidence into the element where the future waited to shape their days.

At that moment Lady Swale, newly awake, lay in bed and watched the slow growing light of dawn through her half-drawn curtains. Another day . . . the same routine . . . years ahead of her that she could with more or less accuracy broadly detail. Well, perhaps so much of her dissatisfaction had sprung, if not from her own faults, at least from her own lack of spirit. Some people got what they wanted because they went for it — like her husband. Others got what they little valued because they had stood and let things happen to them. She was lost because she had no true spirit and no courage which sprang from deep self-respect. She lived in a cage and the unmoving conviction was full grown in her that even if one day the cage door were left open then she would still rest the victim of her own deep timidity and would stay within the gilded bars of her comfortable prison.

In a few weeks' time Richard Crane would be leaving. She was free to go with him, but she knew she would never bring herself to the point of going. She sighed and fell into a deep reverie, willed herself into it to find comfort, going back over the years to late girlhood and early womanhood, to the immature love affairs and flirtations that had enriched her days. Well . . . she soothed herself . . . for everything there was a time and a place but for her to escape they had both been long ago offered and were now past recall. She was now a shadow, a ghost that haunted Swale Place, and a poor one neither frightening nor exciting anyone. Perhaps that was why her husband abused her, to see if he could awake some hidden spirit in her, some defiant *alter ego*. Maybe . . . maybe, yes. Maybe that was some part of a love for her in him which she had never suspected. Libertine he might be — but it perhaps arose because she had never discovered that all those years ago deep in her nature was a large element of prudery, of affected modesty which he had too extravagantly and forcefully tried to abolish. More than once she had called him brute to his face — but there could never have been any truth in that because the things in his great cellars and his donations to museums proved him a highly civilized man . . . or did it? God knew . . . and all she knew at the moment was that given all the freedom in the world to choose to be what she would, to go where she would, to love whom she would, she feared that a hidden core of helplessness and indecision would find her unequal to the simple problem of making a choice. She had grown into Swale Place like the ivy that grew on its walls. She liked her cage and would stay in it. Only an earthquake could make her flee from the place . . . only some act of providence . . . of God . . . of shattering upheaval . . .

★ ★ ★

The man was dead. He had never seen him before. Could place a possible reason for the act . . . some fanatic bird lover. But in God's name, to take a rifle to him . . . God rot his soul and who cared a damn! All thought now was for himself. The bullet had taken him high through the left shoulder and he was bleeding steadily but — and his calmness surprised him as he made his survey — not from an arterial rupture. Sitting up he took the scarf from round his neck, wadded it into a pad and thrust it inside his shirt to staunch the wound. He got slowly to his feet, picked up the rifle and the sack he had brought for the birds . . . the birds which had flown. But that now was the least of his troubles — there were other days and other gifts.

In the growing light he looked down at the man and shook his head. He looked ordinary enough, common, and, the fleeting thought made his lips tighten and curl with a flicker of amusement even in his own trouble, was unlikely to have been some husband he had cuckolded.

He walked away along the high pebble ridge towards his car, and already his mind was beginning to throw up suggestions and as quickly reject them. He had to have a story that would hold water. He had lain there after the bullet had spun him round and down and, even to his surprise in that surprising moment, he had found intuition and intelligence linked so that he had become detached from himself and could stand back and direct his own destiny in the coming minutes. The man would come to make sure he was dead . . . to leave him wounded and to survive would be an idiocy. So let him come. His right hand had closed around the largest of the beach stones he could find . . . the bastard, the bastard. There was going to be a mess and there was going to be a lot of talk and . . . well, he had to have a story, his story . . . His mind worked on it all the way to the Rolls-Royce.

He opened the car door, tossed the rifle and the sack in the back and then got in himself. He handled the wheel and knew that he could drive easily on the automatic setting. But the real problem was his story . . . It had to be good . . . or good enough . . . He smiled thinly. He had all the advantages and knew how to take them, whilst that unknown bugger out there . . . fanatic . . . had no one to say a word for him. But . . . one thing he saw he would have to be able to answer and that was — what was he doing close before dawn on the pebble beach below Hurlstone Point?

It had to be good. It had to be good. And he had to have it ready before he drove off to find the nearest telephone box and call his doctor. If he could he must keep dark his intention to take the birds. Bloody bad for his image . . .

Now, what in hell was he to say? That he hadn't been able to sleep? That he had decided to go for a drive? That this . . . that that . . . He ran through the alternatives . . . This was big trouble unless he was convincing. By Christ it had to be good . . . Deep in thought, mulling over the story to tell, and harassed, too, by the not too urgent but real need to get to a doctor, he lapsed into complete concentration.

Outside the car the day was growing and a slight mist was rising from the meadow across which Alfie Grey had walked to the pebble ridge. High over Hurlstone Point the two adult peregrine falcons circled and called. In a little while the courage would come to their young to take fully to the air . . .

269

And it was in concentrating on his own, if not survival then public standing and the protection of his good name, that Sir Anthony Swale — from ingrained habit — reached out and took without conscious knowledge of doing so, the packet of cigarettes which Steve Black had left in the dashboard compartment. He opened it, holding it in the hand of his injured arm, took a cigarette, and put it into his mouth. Almost unknowingly, deep in thought, his eyes on the sea, on the rollers running, foam-crested into the beach, and the noise of the suck and surge of the breaking waves on the pebbles clear in the still morning air, he reached out and pressed the plunger of the dashboard cigarette lighter.

The sound of the explosion sent every bird in the area either into the air or crouching instantly into immobility. It set the two young falcons into their first full flight. As they flew clear of the cliff they breasted a strengthening north-easterly breeze and began to climb to join the parent birds still above them.

Other titles published by
The House of Ulverscroft:

TALES OF MYSTERY AND HORROR: VOL.III

Edgar Allan Poe

These *Tales of Mystery and Horror* include the story of Bedloe, a wealthy young invalid, who has a strange tale to tell his physician, after he experiences a form of time travel, in *A Tale of The Ragged Mountains* . . . And *The Conversation of Eiros and Charmion* is a very strange tale of a comet approaching earth, causing it to contain pure oxygen. The result of this has a devastating effect on people . . .